My Name is Erin, and My Mom's an Addict

D1453554

by
Amy Voltaire

Blue Dragon Publishing

My Name is Erin, and My Mom's an Addict

By Amy E. Voltaire

Published by Blue Dragon Publishing, LLC

PO Box 247

Lightfoot, VA 23090

Copyright © 2019 by Amy Voltaire

ISBN 978-1-939696-49-6 (paperback)

ISBN 978-1-939696-50-2 (ebook)

Library of Congress Control Number: 2019932496

YAF058080 Social Themes/Drugs, Alcohol, Substance Abuse

Cover by: Resa Reid

Dedication

For my sister, Lydia. Thank you for being my best friend, for always being *by* my side and *on* my side. You are my constant, my season in the sun, and I forgive you for all the bad haircuts.

Special thanks to:

Erika St. Dennis, you are remarkable!

Chase, I never thought the day would come that I would be receiving feedback, advice, and constructive criticism from my child, but it looks like that day has arrived. Thanks for being honest. I love you.

Chapter One

When I was five, our school bus driver was Mrs. Peese. You can imagine how much fun a bunch of little kids had with that name. That fateful day, when she pulled up to the bus stop and opened the creaky bus doors, I was the first kid to hit the steps. Behind me were the other two kids who got off at our stop—my friend Katy Spears, also five, and her big brother, Kyle.

As usual, Katy's mom was at the stop waiting. Each morning, she brought Katy and Kyle to the bus stop, waiting with them for the bus. And each afternoon, she was waiting when the bus brought them back. My mom didn't take me to the bus stop or wait for me to come home. She said I was a big girl, and besides, Mrs. Spears would look after me. Also, my mom slept a lot. When she wasn't sleeping, she had friends who came over to visit, and they'd go in her room with the door locked. So, she didn't do the whole bus stop thing.

My feet hit the ground and I bolted, almost plowing right into Mrs. Spears.

"Whoa, Erin! You almost ran me over! What's the hurry?" she asked.

I kept running and yelled without looking back, "I'm going home to see my new puppy!"

"Oh! A new puppy! How wonderful!" she called out.

I didn't acknowledge her as I ran towards our trailer, which was about a minute up the road. I wasn't really in a hurry because of my new puppy. I was in a hurry because I had to use the bathroom so badly that I thought I might pee on myself.

In fact, there was no puppy; that was a lie. Maybe I lied because I really, really wanted a puppy. I asked my mom for one at least weekly, and every week she'd said the same thing. "Erin, how many times do I have to tell you that pets are against the trailer park's rules?"

I always had a remedy. We could get a tiny dog and keep him inside. Nobody would ever know he was there.

"Tiny dogs bark too, Erin. People would hear the dog, they'd tell on us, and then we'd be in big trouble. They might kick us out. Then what would we do? We'd be homeless," Mom would say.

I didn't believe that even the meanest landlord would kick someone out over a puppy. After all, who doesn't love puppies?

"But we could train him to be quiet."

"You can't train a dog to be quiet. Barking is what dogs do." Mom always won the puppy argument, but that never stopped me from asking again. I'd asked before I left for school that morning, and she'd yelled at me.

I finally made it up the wooden porch and to the door. I did the pee dance as I tried to turn the knob. It wouldn't turn. This was not good. Maybe I wasn't turning hard enough. I tried again. Still a no-go. I banged on the door and waited a few seconds, but Mom didn't come. Maybe she was sleeping. I banged harder.

"I GOTTA PEEEEEE!" I yelled. *Mrs. Peese pees, and I'm about to pee my pants,* ran through my head. No answer. I ran down the porch steps, pulled my pants down, and went in the grass. I knew I would be in trouble if my mom saw me, but it was that or go all over myself, and only babies were supposed to do that. I looked around and saw no one outside. When I was finished, I pulled my pants up and marched back up to the front door.

This time I didn't knock as urgently, but still hard enough that she would hear it. We didn't have a car, and there were no cars in the driveway, so she wasn't busy with visitors. If she was sleeping, the loud knocking would rouse her.

Maybe Mr. Jim, one of her friends, had taken her to the store in his green car. Or maybe she'd gone somewhere with her other friend in Tiff's little red car. I sat down on the top step and waited.

After what felt like an eternity, but was probably closer to an hour, I started to get scared. She'd never been gone like this before. What if she was gone forever? I didn't know anyone whose mom had left forever, but that didn't mean it couldn't happen. *I'm a good girl, so she wouldn't leave me,* I thought. Maybe she was mad at me for asking for a puppy again that morning.

The longer I sat there and went over the possible scenarios, the more terrified I became. I decided I'd never ask for a puppy again. As soon as she got home, I would give her the biggest hug I could give. I'd tell her how much I loved her and give her kisses. *She'll be back soon,*

I told myself. *My mommy wouldn't leave me just because I asked for a puppy.*

No, of course, she wouldn't leave because of that.

She'd leave because, as I found out later, she was a heroin addict.

Chapter Two

Looking back, I realize it was a good thing that I told that lie to Mrs. Spears. After I'd sat on my porch for what must have been two hours, Mrs. Spears showed up with Katy in tow. They had come to see the new puppy and instead, had discovered me still on the porch, crying. After some time, Mrs. Spears was able to convince me to come home with her and Katy for dinner.

I was glad that I went home with them because I was hungry, and Mrs. Spears ordered pizza. After we finished eating, Katy got up and went to the bathroom, and Mrs. Spears said to me, "Erin, I'm going to go see if your mother is home yet."

"Can I come?" I asked.

"I need you to stay here and help Katy and Mr. Spears clean up the dinner dishes, but if your mom's home, I'll come right back for you. If she's not, I'll leave a note on the door with my phone number, so she can call me when she gets there. How's that sound?"

"Okay," I said, even though I wasn't buying the whole "help clean up" story. We'd only dirtied a few dishes. I may have only been five, but I wasn't an idiot.

Mr. Spears put his plate in the sink, then went around the corner into the hallway and said, "Janice, come here for a sec."

When they started whispering, I got out of my chair and tiptoed near the corner, so I could hear what they were saying.

"What's going on? Why won't you take Erin with you?" Mr. Spears whispered.

"If I take her and her mother's not home, she might refuse to come back with me. It was hard to get her here in the first place. If the poor thing hadn't been so hungry, I doubt she would have agreed to come at all. If her mother is there, I want to see what condition she's in. I've heard she's into some pretty heavy stuff, and if that's true, if she seems messed up, I won't leave Erin with her."

I ran quietly back to my chair and sat down.

They whispered a bit more, and then Mrs. Spears grabbed her purse from the counter. "Be right back, Erin."

I wondered what she meant by "heavy stuff." I'd never seen my mommy lift anything bigger than a bag of trash.

Ten minutes later, Mrs. Spears was back. My mom hadn't come home.

In fact, she never came home. And that was almost ten years ago.

Chapter Three

I'm fifteen years old now, and I know a lot more about everything than I knew on the day my mother left. I live with my father's mom and dad, Trish and Bob Whitaker. Gram and Pap are good people, and I love them a lot, even though they're overprotective.

They're also silly. They were twenty years old when they met at their job, which was (are you ready for this?) at the circus. Yep, my Gram and Pap were in the circus. Oh, it gets better...they were clowns. They actually went to clown school. You won't see any old photos of them at a concert, a portrait studio, or anywhere like that. In their photos, they're in full clown garb. There's even one of them kissing, and Pap is holding one of those horns that clowns honk.

He always says that Gram was the prettiest clown in the circus, and though that is supposed to be a compliment, it doesn't sound like one. Some people might be embarrassed about literally having clowns as relatives, but I think it's pretty cool that both of my grandparents can juggle and ride unicycles.

Of course, they aren't in the circus anymore. Gram got pregnant a few months after they met, and there wasn't much room under the big top for a pregnant clown. Plus, they didn't want their kid to live a gypsy's life, so they quit. Pap got a job as a mail clerk in the county's government office, and now he's the boss of the mail department. I wonder if his coworkers know that he can juggle?

When I first came to stay with Gram and Pap, it had only been a couple of days after my mom left. I was scared. I didn't remember my grandparents because my mom had stopped taking me around them shortly after my dad—their only son—died.

I was only two, so I don't remember him either. He was killed instantly in an accident when a dump truck driver ran a red light and hit his car on the driver's side. Gram has a lot of pictures of my dad, but it feels weird to look at them, because even though he was my dad, it's like looking at a stranger. It makes me sad; not because I miss him (how can you miss someone you don't know?), but because I never knew him.

In the pictures, he looks like he was really nice. He had a huge, bright smile in every single photo. No kidding. There is not one picture where he's not smiling, even in baby photos. I think about how different things might be if it hadn't been for that accident.

When the insurance company paid my mom the claim money, she moved us to another town away from Gram and Pap. She even changed her phone number. Gram and Pap said they missed me terribly and looked but couldn't find me. My mom had basically disappeared.

She bought the trailer home with some of the insurance money, and Pap says she must have shot the rest of it in her arm.

I remember the trailer. It was a dump because my mom didn't take care of it, and she didn't clean. She didn't cook either. We didn't have much food, and the food we did have was mostly things like Pop-Tarts, canned raviolis, and microwave dinners called "Kids' Cookery." My favorites were the chicken nuggets and the pizza. I was a master at pushing the buttons.

I haven't had a microwave dinner since I've been with Gram and Pap. Gram is a fantastic cook. She names her dishes after herself—Gram's Gooey Goulash, Gram's BAM! Beef Stew, Gram's Succulent Spaghetti—you get the picture. When she can't come up with a catchy name, she puts "Gram's" at the beginning of whatever the dish is.

About a week after I came to stay with Gram and Pap, we'd finished eating Gram's Luscious Lasagna, and they decided it was time to let me know some of what was going on. I still remember the conversation.

"You're going to be staying with us for a while, Erin," Gram said.

"I don't want to stay here. I want my mommy."

"Your mommy can't be with you right now. She's sick, honey."

"Did she get hurt picking up something heavy?" I asked with the tears rolling down my cheeks.

"Something heavy?" Pap said.

"Mrs. Spears said Mommy was doing heavy stuff."

"It's not that kind of hurt or sick. It's a different kind of sick," Gram said. As I waited for Gram to tell me what that meant, she looked around like she was waiting for some invisible person to tell her what to say. Apparently nobody did because Pap chimed in.

"Sometimes people do things...like drugs, that make them get sick in their minds, to where they don't think normal. Your momma's mind isn't thinking normal. If her mind was working the way it does when it's not sick, she wouldn't have left you."

"She's not mad at me?" I asked.

"Of course not, sweetheart," Pap said. "She's simply confused."

"Why doesn't she stop the drug-things, so she can stop being confused?" I asked.

"Sometimes people can't stop," Pap said. "People who can't stop doing drugs are called drug addicts."

"Where is she now? Can we go see her? Please?" I asked. I felt the tears falling down my cheeks.

"Honey, we don't know where your momma is," Gram said.

By that time, I was crying so hard that I could barely get the words out. It was the kind of hurt where you can hardly catch your breath.

"But Mrs. Spears left a note, and my mommy is going to call her when she gets home. We need to take a new note because she has the wrong phone number! She has Mrs. Spears's phone number, not yours."

Gram and Pap looked at each other. They both looked sad.

"Erin, honey," Gram said, "your momma knows our phone number. If she needs to get in touch with us, she'll be able to."

I wondered if Gram and Pap just wanted to keep me. I thought maybe my mom wanted me, but they didn't want to give me back. I didn't know what drugs were. I didn't understand what a drug addict was. The only thing I understood was that my mommy wasn't there, and I refused to believe that she didn't want me anymore. In my five-year-old mind, the only logical explanation was that she was being kept from me.

For the next year or so, Gram and Pap tucked me in every night, and each time they turned the light off and left my room, I cried myself to sleep. I didn't trust them.

Chapter Four

That first year was hard. Really hard. Every time the phone rang, I got excited, thinking it was my mom calling to say she felt better and wanted me back. But it never was. I always worried about her and wondered if she was okay. Because she was pretty much all I thought about, I didn't do well in school and had to go to summer school so I wouldn't have to repeat the first grade.

In elementary school, I made up stories about my mom. I told other kids that she was working in another country, and that she would be back to get me soon. We were going to travel the world together, and I was going to learn to speak in other languages.

I doubt it was easy for Gram and Pap. They didn't expect to have another child to raise. Pap said I have always been a handful. I guess I did have a bit of a mean streak. Sometimes I'd say hurtful things to them, which I heard Pap say wasn't surprising after all I'd been through. That made me angrier.

At some point, I finally stopped obsessing about my mom. The phone would ring, and I no longer stopped what I was doing to run over and eavesdrop on the call. I did better in school, and I had friends there, so I didn't mind going. I was invited to a few birthday parties, but the other kids whispered about me when Gram stayed to visit with the other parents. Everyone thought she was too old to be my mother. I didn't want to explain that my mom was sick, and no one believed she was traveling for work anymore. Pretty soon I stopped going.

At least in the trailer park, there were a few kids for me to play with outside of school, but not at my new house. We live in a brick rancher on an acre of land, right off a mile-long road that runs into the main street. There were only five other houses on our street, and since none of the people in those houses had kids, there was nobody for me to hang around with after school. When I wasn't at school, I mostly played alone.

Sometimes, Gram and Pap played board games with me, and we watched movies. There were a few kids at school that I liked okay, but I wasn't close enough to them that I would ever feel comfortable telling them anything about my family situation. In fact, I'd never had anyone over to spend the night or spent the night away until I was fourteen. That's when I met Grace.

I really liked my ninth grade English teacher, Mr. Thompson. He was younger than a lot of the other teachers in our school, probably mid- or late twenties. I think since he was closer to our age, he understood us more than the older teachers did. He didn't treat us like a bunch of dumb kids. But the most important reason I liked him was because he assigned seats.

Most of the time, instead of liking a teacher for that reason, I'd feel the opposite. But because of Mr.

Thompson's assigned seats, I ended up next to Grace, who became my best friend. If it hadn't been for him and his assigned seats, I wouldn't have her. Oh, and I also have Jimmy Howes to thank for that.

Jimmy Howes was the class clown in English from the very first day. As soon as he was assigned his seat, which happened to be next to mine, he started with the complaining.

"Can I switch seats?" he asked Mr. Thompson. "This one's not gonna work for me."

"What's the problem with your seat, Mr....," Mr. Thompson looked at his seating chart and continued, "James Howes?"

"My name's Jimmy," he said. Then, he looked straight at me. "I don't like the view."

I felt my ears get hot with embarrassment. I think Mr. Thompson knew that Jimmy was implying that I was ugly, so Mr. Thompson gave him a dirty look.

When Jimmy saw that look, he instantly tried to backpedal. "There's no view here. I want to be next to the window where I can see outside."

"Well, luckily for you, the only two things you need to be able to see are me and the board. I trust that you can see me? And the board?" Mr. Thompson asked.

"Yeah, but there's also a draft right here. I get strep throat a lot, and I'm not supposed to be in drafty areas."

Everyone knew that Jimmy was full of crap. Especially Mr. Thompson. But Mr. Thompson wasn't going to let him win. This was the first day of class, and the teacher has to establish rank with some smart-aleck kid on the first day. As Pap always said, "There's always one in the bunch."

Mr. Thompson looked at Jimmy for a few seconds. "Your classmates have settled in already, so I'm not going to ask anyone to move." Then, addressing the whole class, he said, "However, if anyone would like to switch seats with Mr. Howes, please raise your hand."

A pretty girl with long, brown hair raised her hand. "I'll switch with him."

"Very well, and thank you,..." and then after checking the chart again, "Ms. Mills. Grace Mills."

Grace and Jimmy switched seats. She sat down and looked at me. "That Jimmy guy is a douche-bag, and you look like a decent person. I couldn't let you get stuck with him for an entire school year."

I liked her right away. "Thanks," I said, smiling.

Mr. Thompson gave us the rundown of his classroom rules. Be respectful to your teacher and peers. Participate. No phones out while he was teaching or during tests or quizzes, but when we got our work done, we could, as he put it, "Quietly indulge in cellular activities. PG-rated sites only and do not disturb your classmates who are still working." The whole class cheered about being able to use cell phones. Except for me. I didn't have a cell phone.

He gave us a syllabus and went over it. "The first day of the school year is special because I not only permit, but encourage, socializing rather than working. No homework tonight either. Talk quietly amongst yourselves for the rest of the class and enjoy. Next class, please come prepared to dive into English."

Grace turned to me. "I like Mr. Thompson. He's so nice."

Based on the look on her face, I suspected Grace had a crush on Mr. Thompson. He *was* cute.

"Yeah, he seems pretty great. Thanks for volunteering to switch with Jimmy."

"No problem. He's obnoxious."

"How come I don't remember you from last year?"

Grace smiled. "Because I went to private school."

"Are you rich or something?" I asked.

She didn't seem offended. Instead, she started laughing. "That's funny! No, I didn't go to some upscale rich girls' school. I went to Zimmerman's, which in my opinion is a glorified daycare. I mean, it's school, but they also have babies there. There were only nineteen students in the eighth-grade class last year. I've been going since I was little because both of my parents worked."

"Oh. Where do they work?"

"My dad's an accountant. My mom was a counselor, but she died when I was ten."

"Wow. I'm sorry."

"It's fine."

I looked down at my fingernails, pretending to be looking for something in particular. I didn't know what to say. I wanted to ask Grace how her mom died, but I didn't want to be nosy. For a second, I wondered if her mom overdosed, which made me realize how pathetic it was that drugs were first thing to come to my mind when the subject of death came up. Next, I thought about my mom and how I missed her, but at the same time, I never wanted to see her again.

Grace interrupted my thoughts. "Do you want to hang out sometime after school?"

"Sure." I tried not to show too much excitement. If we ended up being friends, she'd figure out soon enough that I'd never had a real friend.

"Why don't you call and ask your mom if you can spend the night Friday? I promise that we're normal. We don't have people buried in our basement or anything. Actually, we don't have a basement. I could get my dad to call her if you want."

I didn't want to tell her about my mom. It's kind of embarrassing when people find out that your parent is a heroin addict. Although, when I first found out and didn't understand it, I would tell perfect strangers. One time, Gram took me to the 7-11 for a Slurpee, and when we got to the counter, I told the cashier, "My mommy ran away because she's an attic."

I didn't know what the word addict meant until I was about ten. It didn't seem right that my mom was the one to abandon me so she could stick needles in her arms, yet I was the one feeling embarrassed. I hoped that wherever she was, she felt embarrassed, ashamed, and guilty.

"I live with my grandparents. My dad died when I was two, and my mom isn't around." *There,* I thought, *I was honest without telling everything.* "Your dad can call my grandma though." I really wanted Grace to get to like me before she found out my mother was a junkie.

"Where's your mom?"

So much for that, I thought. I took a deep breath.

"She took off when I was five. Drugs."

"Oh. That sucks. Well, give me your grandma's phone number, and I'll get my dad to call her tonight."

So, that was it? She hadn't blinked an eye. She didn't look disgusted or shocked. I expected her to react the way someone would react if you tell them you have a highly contagious and deadly disease, but it was nothing like that. It was nice to know that Grace wasn't judgmental. Maybe if we became good friends, I'd actually have someone my age that I could talk to about my mom. I was excited for Friday to come.

Chapter Five

It had been years since I got excited when our house phone rang. When Grace's dad called, I was sitting at the kitchen table doing math homework. Gram walked around me to get to the phone. I had told her about Grace and let her know that Mr. Mills might be calling. She picked up on the third ring.

"Hello? Yes. Yes, Erin told me about Grace. That would be fine." She paused. "Oh yes, Erin is thrilled." Gram looked at me and gave me an excited smile.

"Okay, let me grab a pen and paper so I can get your address." Another pause while she got her pen out. "No, that's fine, we don't mind bringing her. I'm ready. What's your address? Mmm-hmm. Got it. What time would you like for us to bring her? Sounds good. We look forward to meeting you, Mr. Mills. Bye-bye."

Gram hung the phone up and patted me on the shoulder. "It's so nice that you made a friend today, Erin. What do you girls plan to do at the sleepover?"

"I don't know Gram. I've never spent the night at anyone's house, and we didn't really talk about what we were going to do."

"Well, when I was a girl and had sleepovers with my friends, we did each other's hair and talked about boys. We gave each other makeovers and manicures and talked about boys. We ate junk food and talked about boys. Sometimes we called boys and then hung up when they answered the phone. Sleepovers were so much fun." Gram is sweet, but she is also annoying sometimes.

I couldn't see Grace and me talking about boys, and I definitely couldn't imagine calling a boy and then hanging up on him when he answered the phone. To me, that's stupid. I also didn't think we'd be playing around with makeup or hair. Grace didn't look like she wore makeup, and her brown hair was straight and all one length. Mine was much lighter but just as straight. The only thing close to makeup that I had was a tube of Chapstick. I didn't know if Grace was into that kind of stuff. If she were, I'd try it out to make her happy.

"I don't think we'll be calling any boys, Gram," I said.

"What's this about boys?" Pap asked as he came in and opened the refrigerator.

"Erin is going to a sleepover on Friday," Gram announced.

"With boys?" Pap asked.

"No, Pap. Just my friend Grace. Gram thinks we'll be calling boys, but we're not."

"Okay. Don't make me get my shotgun out," Pap said, and then laughed like he had told the best joke ever.

Pap doesn't own a shotgun. I didn't call him out on that, or the fact that the whole shotgun joke was the oldest and probably worst joke in history. Instead, I smiled and shook my head. I never have thought that clowns were funny, but I love my Gram and Pap, so I pretend to like their cheesy jokes.

Chapter Six

I was super excited about Friday, so the rest of the week went by pretty slowly. After Gram had talked about doing makeup and calling boys, I started to wonder what we actually would be doing. What was supposed to happen at sleepovers? I mean, what was the point of them anyway? Does something special happen when you sleep over at someone's house that doesn't happen when you go over to visit for a few hours?

I remembered how strange it felt when I first got to Gram and Pap's and had to sleep in my room for the first time. It wasn't technically my room yet; it was Gram's special room where she kept her collectible clown figurines. I'm talking at least two hundred of them. The room was painted an ugly color of pink that reminded me of Pepto Bismol. There was a bed in there, but the rest of the furniture consisted of glass cabinets that were full of clowns collecting dust.

Luckily, though I don't think clowns are funny, I've never been afraid of them. It was scary enough to be away from my own bed and my mom, so it would have been terrifying if I were afraid of clowns too.

By the time I had been here a month, Gram had boxed up the clowns and put them in the attic. Pap painted the room a nice shade of green, and they bought me a dresser, nightstand, and a desk with a chair. They bought me some stuffed animals and a comforter set with pink and green flowers all over it. Pap put a full-length mirror on the back of my door. He said, "A girl as pretty as you needs to be able to see the pretty from head to toe."

Pap always says nice things like that. I don't know if he really thinks I'm pretty, or if he says that to make me feel good. He's probably just trying to make me feel good. If I was pretty, Jimmy Howes wouldn't have asked for a window seat.

On Wednesday, Mr. Thompson gave us our first writing assignment. "I want you to make up a character and write a short paragraph about him or her. Don't tell me what the character looks like; I want to know how that character feels, how they think, how they act. What are the character's hopes and dreams? What are his or her likes and dislikes?"

"My character dislikes English class," Jimmy Howes said. "He thinks it's the dumbest class in school."

Mr. Thompson wasn't fazed. "Great! You're already thinking about who your character is. I'm glad you're so enthusiastic about this assignment. But your job is to write about him, Jimmy, not speak out loud about him."

Grace looked at me and smiled. Mr. Thompson was awesome. He liked all of us, even Jimmy Howes. I don't know why anyone would like Jimmy, but Mr. Thompson did—or maybe he just faked it really well. He wrote our assignment on the board, and we copied it down. He put a smiley face underneath and turned to us. "This is due Friday. I'm excited to meet your characters, a.k.a., your new friends...or maybe foes."

I started on my assignment as soon as I got home. I liked the idea of making up a person. It could be a girl or a guy. They could be young or old, beautiful or unattractive, smart or stupid. The possibilities were endless. In the end, my character Kit (I've always liked that name) ended up being like me in some ways but also some of what I wanted to be. When I finished writing, I read it over and was pretty pleased with my new friend.

Meet Kit. She's twenty-five years old. There are a few things you should know about her. She's a total badass with a quick temper, a black belt, and a gun, so I advise you not to piss her off. The good news is that it takes a lot to piss her off, so unless you're in the business of dealing or manufacturing drugs (these are the things that REALLY make her mad), you're probably safe. You see, Kit's a DEA agent. You're probably wondering why she chose that profession, so I'll enlighten you. Kit grew up in a drug-infested neighborhood and saw a lot of people die, not only from using drugs, but also in drug-related shootings. One of those people was her uncle, who was an innocent bystander in a drug-related robbery at the convenience store where he worked. Kit was close to her uncle, and on the day of his funeral, Kit vowed to devote her life to taking dealers down, and now she's fulfilling that vow. Kit may be tough on the outside, but she's got a big heart and loves little kids and animals.

Chapter Seven

Although our assignment wasn't due until Friday, I turned mine in the next day. Mr. Thompson seemed impressed that I'd turned it in early, which made me feel good because I liked him, and I wanted him to like me. I enjoyed his class because we were allowed to have fun. You would think that if a teacher lets kids have fun, the class would end up being like a zoo, but it was the opposite. Because we didn't want him to change how he ran his classroom, we followed the rules. If we made his job easy, he'd keep being awesome. I think he knew that, and I also think that's why he was the smartest teacher at school.

When the bell rang on Friday, Mr. Thompson said, "Erin, can I see you for a minute, please?"

Uh-oh, I thought. I knew that writing "ass" and "piss" might not be a good idea, but I had done it anyway because Kit really was a badass, and you didn't want to piss her off.

I was shocked when he handed me my paper and said, "I like your character a lot, Erin."

I looked at the paper, and the grade was written at the top in marker. He'd given me an A!

"Thank you, Mr. Thompson. I thought maybe I was in trouble."

"Why would you be in trouble?" he asked.

"Because of ass and piss. I just thought..."

"Actually, though you probably shouldn't use such colorful language for a school assignment, that is one of the reasons I liked it."

I must have looked confused because he asked, "Kit is a ninja, right? A total badass that nobody messes with?"

"Yeah, she is."

"Well, you used the words that you felt described her most accurately. You didn't use those words for the sake of using them. You used them because you were being honest, and you were trying to tell me about Kit, exactly as you imagined her. Right?"

"Yeah."

"I like that. In the future though, let's go ahead and try to find other words that aren't so iffy for school submissions." He looked around as if he was checking to make sure that nobody was in the room. "Even though if it were up to me, I'd be fine with any words you use as long as they are honest. Good work, young lady. I think you've got some talent, and I look forward to reading more."

I walked out of that class feeling fantastic. I had never felt that way before. *Is this how drugs make you feel?* I wondered. If so, I understood why people would want to feel this way all the time.

I can't believe that my mind always ties everything back to drugs! I thought. *I need to get over that.*

Mr. Thompson thought I was talented! Nobody had ever said anything like that to me. Sure, Pap and Gram said nice things, but they're my grandparents, so I think they feel like they have to. But Mr. Thompson didn't have to say nice things. As I walked to my next class, I found myself thinking about and looking forward to our next writing assignment.

Gram was boiling noodles for her Gooey Goulash when I got home. I got the assignment out of my book bag and set it down on the kitchen table. "Look, Gram."

"An A! Very good!"

She picked it up and read it. I waited patiently for her to finish. Gram was a slow reader.

"Hey, that's good, Erin. That Kit sounds like something else."

"She is! Mr. Thompson really liked it, Gram. He thinks I have talent."

"Your father was a good writer. I think you may be a chip off the old block! I'll have to go through and find some of the things that he wrote and give them to you."

I realized then that I didn't know very much about my dad. On the way to my bedroom, I grabbed the photo album that Gram kept on the bookcase in the living room. It had pictures of my dad, pictures of me with my dad, and some with my mom in them too. I hadn't looked at them in a long time, and I wanted to look at the ones of my dad again. I took the album in my room and set it on my dresser. I packed a bag to take to Grace's.

When I was done, I sat down on my bed with the photo album. The first few pages had pictures of my dad when he was a baby. I flipped through the pages until I came to the ones that had pictures of him after I was born. I pulled three pictures out of the plastic pockets and put them in the bag: a picture of me with my dad and mom, a picture of Dad and me, and a picture of just my dad. I didn't know if I'd want to show them to Grace, but I'd take them just in case.

Gram knocked on my door and then opened it. "Dinner's ready."

"I'm coming." I waited until she got halfway down the hall before picking up the album. I put it back on the shelf on my way to the kitchen. I didn't want her to know that I was taking the pictures to Grace's. She wouldn't mind if I took them, but she might think I wanted to talk about my dad.

I didn't. Not then, anyway.

Chapter Eight

Grace's house was in a neighborhood called Woods' Edge. I thought that was a strange name for it because there were no woods around. The houses were close together. If you walked out Grace's front door, turned left or right, and walked for ten seconds, you'd be in a neighbor's yard.

The houses were all two-story and had neat, green lawns. Some had pretty bushes and flowers, but Grace's yard just had grass. You could see where there'd been a flowerbed on either side of the front porch, but now it was filled with weeds. I wondered if the flowerbeds looked pretty while her mom was still alive.

Gram and Pap insisted on walking me to the house. Before we could ring the bell, Mr. Mills opened the door.

"Ed Mills," he said as he shook Pap's hand, then Gram's.

"I'm Bob Whitaker, and this is my wife, Trish. And this, of course, is Erin," he said putting his hand on my shoulder.

"Please, come in," Mr. Mills said, opening the door wide to let us in.

Just then, Grace appeared. "Hi, Mr. and Mrs. Whitaker. Thanks for letting Erin stay."

"Thank you both for having her," Gram said.

Grace grabbed my hand, pulling me towards the stairs. "Come on, Erin. Let's put your bag in my room."

I was surprised to see that Grace's room was pink and frilly. As if she'd read my mind, she said, "My mom and I bought this stuff right before she got sick. Since we picked it out together, I don't want to change it even though I'm not into pink anymore."

"I don't blame you," I said, setting my bag down.

She had a television, a DVD player, and a bookshelf that was crammed with DVDs.

"Wow, you've got a really nice room."

She shrugged. "Thanks. Everything my dad watches on TV is boring, so if I want to watch something other than sports, I have to watch it in here."

I walked over to look at the DVDs.

"See any you want to watch? We can watch whatever you want. Dad said he'll order pizza for us too."

I didn't see any makeup lying around. "Gram said that girls do makeovers and call boys at sleepovers, but that was when she was young. Is that still what people do or what?"

Grace laughed. "It's been a long time since I've had anyone spend the night. Before my mom got sick, if I had a friend spend the night, my mom would do stuff with us, like bake cookies, do crafts, that sort of thing. When she got sick, I stopped having friends over, and after she died, I just kind of kept to myself, so I'm pretty clueless about what people do at sleepovers. I guess whatever we feel like doing. We can watch a movie or play a board game. I have Monopoly, and we're definitely going to eat pizza. What do you want to do?"

"A movie and pizza sounds good to me. I've never played Monopoly. Is it fun?"

"My dad hates it. My mom didn't like it either but if I begged enough, she'd play. I think it's a great game. We can play it tonight, or we can wait and play another night. For now, pick a movie."

"How about this one?" I asked, holding up a movie called *The Princess Diaries*.

"Oh, I love that movie," Grace said.

The movie was good, though I missed some parts because we talked a lot during it. We ate the whole pizza, and when the movie was over, we were miserably full. I hadn't felt that happy in a long time.

"Wanna call some boys?" Grace asked.

"Only if we can hang up on them when they answer," I said.

"Huh?"

"Gram said that when they called boys, they hung up when they answered the phone."

"What's the point? I don't get it."

"I don't either. I don't even know any boys to call," I admitted.

"I was just kidding. I know some, but I don't have their phone numbers or want to talk to them. If I was going to call any boy, it would be Jimmy Howes."

"Ew, why?" I asked, surprised.

"To hang up on him, of course."

I don't know why, but I found that hilarious and got to laughing. I laughed so hard that my stomach hurt, and tears were running down my face. Grace was laughing at me laughing, and the more she laughed, the more I laughed.

When we finally stopped laughing, I looked over and saw the picture on her nightstand. "Is that your mom?"

"Yeah."

"She was pretty. You look just like her."

"You think so?"

"Definitely."

"Thanks," Grace said, picking up the picture. She ran her finger over her mother's cheek.

I figured if we were going to be friends, it would be okay to ask about her mom. "How'd she die?"

"Cancer. I miss her so much. Do you miss your mom?"

"Yeah, sometimes."

"How old were you when she left?"

"Five."

"What happened?"

"Eh, I don't really like to talk about it." Part of me desperately wanted to tell Grace everything. I knew it would feel good to get it off my chest, and even though I barely knew her, my gut told me I could trust her; but I also didn't want to cry in front of her.

"I don't talk about my mom to anyone, either," she said. "Sometimes talking about her makes me cry and that's embarrassing."

"Exactly," I said. Then, before I could stop myself, I said, "I came home from school one day, and she was just gone. Haven't seen her or heard from her since. I hate her for that. How can a mother just leave a little kid?" I felt my eyes start to well up, so I tried to change the subject. "I brought a couple of pictures of my dad. Wanna see them?"

"Sure," Grace said.

I pulled out two of the three pictures from my bag. I didn't want to look at the one with my mom in it. I handed them to Grace.

"Oh, he was cute!" Grace said.

"Yeah, I think so. He died when I was two, so I don't remember him."

Grace looked at the second picture. "Aw, you were cute too," she said, handing both pictures back to me.

I put them back in my bag. Neither one of us said anything for a few seconds. Then Grace grabbed my hand. "Erin, I'm sorry your mom did such a crappy thing to you."

"Eh, it is what it is. I'm sorry for you way more than I am for me. Your mom was good, and she loved you. I'll bet she would have never left you. I mean, I know she did, but not on purpose. She didn't choose to leave you. People say addiction is a disease. I call bullshit on that. What your mom had...that's a disease. It's not fair that your mom died while my mom is alive somewhere, probably not far from here; she's alive and well, and probably sticking a needle in her arm right now."

Although I'd desperately tried to keep from crying, tears began rolling down my face. Grace put her arms around me and held me tight. It felt nice. Gram and Pap hugged me all the time, but it felt different with Grace.

She was my friend, and she was the only person my age that had any idea how I felt.

"I think I snotted on your shoulder," I said, as I pulled away. "Sorry."

"That's okay. I snotted in your hair," she said. She'd been crying too. I ran my hand over my head, and sure enough, it was wet.

"Ew, you did snot in my hair!" I said. This brought on another laughing fit. We laughed until, exhausted, we fell asleep.

Chapter Nine

I opened my eyes and looked around, seeing nothing familiar. I rolled over, and when I saw Grace's face, I remembered where I was. She was snoring. I lay there looking at her and thinking about how pretty she was. I remembered that I used to do the same thing with my mom.

She'd be asleep on the couch, and I would get close to her and just stare. I'd look at every part of her face, and sometimes I would run my finger across her cheek like Grace had done with her mother's picture the night before. If I touched my mom's lips, she would scratch them with her teeth. I reached out slowly and gently ran my finger over Grace's lip. She swatted at my hand and opened her eyes. She looked really confused for a few seconds. I started laughing.

"Sorry," I said. "I wanted to see if you would scratch your lips with your teeth."

"You're a weirdo. Come on, weirdo friend," she said, sitting up. "Let's go downstairs and make some breakfast."

Grace made pancakes and bacon. I was impressed. "Hey, you're a good cook."

"My mom taught me. Before she got sick, we made breakfast every Saturday and Sunday."

I thought about what it would be like to cook with my mom. I wondered if she knew how to cook anything other than a microwave dinner. I doubted it.

We finished our food and cleaned up the dishes. A few minutes later, Mr. Mills came in the front door and said, "Erin, your parents are here."

I didn't correct him. A lot of people thought Gram and Pap were my parents, and they kind of were.

"Thanks for letting me stay over, Mr. Mills. I had fun."

"Anytime, sweetie," he said.

I grabbed my bag, and Grace walked me to the door. She gave me a hug and said, "See you at school, weirdo."

Chapter Ten

I invited Grace over to spend the night at my house the next weekend. We ordered pizza again. When Gram came in with the food, she handed me a Rite Aid bag.

"You girls can't have a sleep-over without makeup involved. It's un-American."

As I took each item out of the bag and held it up for Grace to see, Gram named it. "That's blush. Lipstick."

"Gram, I've known what lipstick is since I was four."

She ignored me and kept naming the items. We had mascara, lipstick, blush, eyeliner, and eye shadow. Gram asked if we wanted her to show us how to apply everything, but we said no, we'd figure it out. And, boy, did we figure it out!

We went into my room and shut the door. I did Grace's makeup, and she did mine. We looked ridiculous. I don't think I've ever laughed so hard in my entire life. We walked into the living room pretending we were models on the catwalk. Pap was engrossed in something on TV.

"Pap, do we look like models?" I asked, holding back a giggle.

The look on his face was priceless. He thought we were serious and pretended to be impressed. "Well, it looks like y'all gave it the old college try. Nice job for a first time. Maybe Gram can give you a few pointers for next time. Say...you girls don't plan on going anywhere tonight, do ya?"

Grace and I both burst out laughing.

Gram came in, took one look at us, and said, "No, they're not going anywhere looking like that. Come on, girls, let's get those faces washed, and we'll start from scratch."

Once we were all fresh-faced, Gram did our makeup for us, giving a quick tutorial of the proper application of each item as she went. She did a good job with the makeup and the instructions, which surprised me.

"Wow, Gram, you're a natural," I said.

She looked pleased. "I sure am. I can also do the best clown makeup this side of the Mississippi. Go show Pap."

Pap's reaction was genuine this time. "Well, ain't you a pair of lookers? I definitely need to get the shotgun out now."

The next afternoon, after Grace had gone home and Gram was making dinner, I was sitting in the living room with Pap watching TV. He patted the spot beside him on the couch. "Come here for a sec, Erin. I wanna talk to you."

I sat down beside him. "Yeah, Pap?"

"You know, you really made your Gram feel good last night, letting her spend some time with you and Grace. We both miss your dad, but it's especially hard for her sometimes."

"Pap, you and Gram are the best. I love y'all."

"Well, I know all your friends have younger parents, and it's not easy for you. Gram gets on your nerves sometimes, and I probably do too. You got a raw deal on a lot of things and having grandparents as parents is one of them. I just want you to know that we love you, and you mean the world to us, so letting Gram hang out with you last night was a big deal. You made her real happy."

I leaned against him and put my head on his shoulder. He kissed the top of my head. Neither one of us said anything else. I thought about how things might be if they hadn't taken me in. I decided then that I'd make sure to include Gram every time Grace came over.

Chapter Eleven

Grace and I spent the night at each other's houses almost every weekend after that. We had one tradition that we still haven't given up...pizza. We've never had a sleepover without it. Plain cheese, always. I told Grace what Pap said about including Gram and that I thought we should let her hang out with us for a little while whenever Grace stayed over. Grace was all for it. I think she loved Gram and Pap too. One weekend, we even let Gram put clown makeup on us. It was really fun.

School was tolerable. The only class I liked was English. I kept an A in that class, but the other classes were Bs and Cs. I'm not a math or science person, so not only were those classes boring, they were also hard. Grace is good at math, so she helped me out when I needed it.

Mr. Thompson gave us writing assignments every week in addition to our regular homework. Nobody minded though because they were always short assignments. Later in the school year, we were going to have to do a ten-page story. He said that we would take the pieces of the weekly assignments and make the story out of those pieces. I didn't know how that would pan out, but I trusted he knew what he was doing.

In November, I got a sore throat and had to stay home from school. It hurt so much that I could barely swallow. On the second day I stayed home, it had gotten so bad that I asked Gram and Pap to take me to the doctor. They took me to the urgent care place. Pap calls it "Doc-in-a-Box."

By the time the doctor came into the exam room, my throat hurt so badly that I was crying. He practically rolled his eyes when he said, "Oh, it can't be that bad," which made me feel pretty dumb. Then, he looked at my throat, took a step back and said, "I'm sorry. I can see why you're crying. How long has your throat been hurting?"

"A couple of days."

He swabbed my throat, left the room, and came back a few minutes later. "You have strep throat," he said. He didn't even prescribe an antibiotic. Instead, he gave me a shot of penicillin in my butt, right there in the exam room.

By that night, I was already feeling better, but Gram said that I was probably still contagious and couldn't go to school or to Grace's to spend the night that weekend.

I was pretty bummed about missing my sleepover at Grace's. We always had so much fun. Sometimes we watched movies, sometimes we played Monopoly, but mostly we just talked and laughed. Since that first time, we hadn't talked about our parents. I think we didn't want to spoil things by talking about depressing stuff, but it was nice to know that if I wanted to talk about those things, I could. Grace understood me, and I understood her.

I felt like our friendship was different from most girls our age. Girls at school seemed to only care about clothes, hair, and boys. Grace and I didn't worry about clothes and hair, but we eventually did start caring about boys. Well, not all boys...just two.

George Barnes was in my science class. Our classroom had tall, long tables with built-in sinks and tall stools instead of chairs. George sat on the stool beside mine. He had messy, brown hair. I hadn't noticed him at first because there wasn't anything special about the way he looked. He was nice, but to me, he was just another guy. Until the first time I heard him laugh.

Class hadn't started yet, so he had his cell phone out. I don't know what got him laughing so hard, but whatever it was, I'm glad he saw it. I heard that laugh, and that was it for me. It was a big, hearty laugh—the kind that would make anyone in earshot laugh along. It made me think about my dad. I had no idea what my dad's laugh sounded like, but when I heard George laugh, I thought, *I'll bet that's how my dad sounded when he laughed.* I would have never thought that you could fall for a person because of the way they laugh, but now I know better.

Grace had a crush on a guy named Jimmy. Not Jimmy Howes, but Jimmy Steiner. When we talked about him, we called him "Good Jimmy." Good Jimmy was in Grace's gym class, and because of that, she was failing gym. She refused to dress out because she didn't want him to see her "ugly, lily-white legs in those dorky gym shorts."

I don't blame her. I don't think gym should be a class, especially not in middle school or high school. The people who decided it should be, must be idiots. If they knew anything about teenagers—which should be a requirement for people who get to decide this kind of stuff—they would know that most of us hate the way we look in our *own* clothes, so what makes them think it's a good idea to make us dress up in those hideous gym clothes?

Grace nailed it when she said they must have had a big meeting where one of them said, "Hey, teenagers are full of self-loathing, but they could use a little more. Let's design the ugliest outfits we can think of and make them parade around in them while sweating."

She did not intend to sweat or wear an ugly outfit, at least not as long as she shared a gym with Good Jimmy. Good Jimmy was incredibly good-looking, but other than that, I'm not sure what Grace saw in him. He was in my math class, and even though he seemed nice enough, he didn't have much of a personality. He definitely didn't compare to George in the laughing department, but then again, nobody ever will.

Because of George and Jimmy, talking about boys became a regular part of our sleepovers. We hadn't sunk to the depths of calling boys and would never sink to the level of hanging up on them, but boys had made it onto the agenda. Grace had a flip phone. Her dad told her that if she was responsible with it, he might get her a smartphone when she turned fifteen. Smartphones were looking more and more enticing. With smartphones, we could download Instagram and if we followed George and

Good Jimmy (after we were already following plenty of other people, of course), we could get a glimpse into their worlds. Christmas was coming, and with both of us being fourteen, we found it reasonable to ask for cell phones.

One night at dinner, I tested the idea out on Gram and Pap.

"Hey, Pap. Do you think fourteen is old enough for a cell phone?"

Gram stopped chewing and looked at Pap.

"Don't know. Never thought about it," he said.

"Most of the kids in my grade have them. Some have had them since they were ten or eleven."

"Are you trying to tell me you want a cell phone, Erin?"

"A smartphone—if they're not too expensive. I don't need the newest version."

Before Pap could answer, Gram chimed in. "No, ma'am," she said.

"Why not?" I asked.

"You're too young," she said, reaching for the salt. Pap kept eating but was watching us intently.

"I told you all the kids at school have them."

"And I said no," she replied.

It wasn't fair, and I was starting to get mad. If she were younger, she'd understand.

"I guess the kids at school have them because they aren't living with people from the last century," I mumbled just loud enough for Gram to hear me.

"Watch it," Gram warned.

I pushed the food around the plate with my fork; I wasn't hungry anymore.

My huffing finally got to Gram. She put her fork down and looked at me. "Erin, not only do I think you're too young, I also know how expensive those phones are."

That really pissed me off. "Don't you get money for me?" I asked. "From the state or something? And aren't you supposed to spend it on me? I never get anything, so you probably owe me at least a phone for all the extra money you're getting."

Gram grabbed me by the arm and yanked me out of my chair.

"OW!"

"Trish...," Pap said.

Gram shot him a look that said he better not interfere. She pulled me into the living room to the bookcase where she finally let my arm loose. She grabbed a three-ring binder from the case and opened it. It was full of bank statements. The one in the front of the binder was the most recent statement, and she pointed to a number on it.

"Do you see this? This is the balance of the account that we opened for you when you came here." It was a *lot* of money. "This is where every bit of money we've ever gotten for you goes. It's for college. So, guess what? Every single penny that's been spent on you has come out of our pockets."

She was fuming. I didn't know what to say and thought it was best to keep my mouth shut. She didn't give me a chance to speak anyway.

"Just carry your ungrateful self to your room. I don't even want to look at you right now."

I went to my room and closed the door. If she hadn't shown me that bank statement, I might have slammed my door, but I knew that would be a terrible idea.

I stood by the door rubbing my arm and listened as Gram and Pap argued. Pap told Gram that she shouldn't have lost her temper with me. Gram told Pap that he babied me.

"And if you keep it up," she said, "you'll ruin her."

I stayed in my room for the rest of the night. By the time I went to bed, I wasn't mad anymore, and when I finally fell asleep, I'd already started feeling guilty. I knew that if it weren't for my grandparents, I'd probably be in foster care. Here they were using their own money to raise me so that they could save up for my college, and I was acting like a total brat.

The next morning, when I went into the kitchen, they were sitting at the table.

"I'm really sorry," I said.

"Forgiven," Gram said, not even looking at me. I could tell she was still mad.

Pap just looked at me and smiled.

After a few days, Gram was back to her normal self, and I was glad; I'd never seen her that mad, and I never wanted to again. I still wanted a cell phone, but I decided I'd better wait at least a year before bringing it up again.

Chapter Twelve

On Saturday, two weeks before Christmas, Grace's dad took us to Walmart to do some Christmas shopping. Gram and Pap gave me twenty-five dollars so that I could buy Grace a present. Grace's dad gave her money too. Grace and I agreed that we wouldn't use the money to buy each other presents. She'd use her money to buy her dad a gift, and my twenty-five bucks would go toward something for Gram and Pap.

It would be hard to keep it a secret though, with Grace's dad going into the store with us, so Grace asked her dad, "When we get there, will you drop us off and go hang out at another store?"

"No way," said Mr. Mills. "There are too many crazies and perverts in the world."

"Daddy, nobody is gonna snatch us from the Walmart in broad daylight."

"You don't know what people will or won't do. Besides, even if I was stupid enough to drop two young girls off in a busy store, do you think Erin's grandparents would appreciate it? I'm not dropping you and Erin off anywhere—case closed."

Grace sighed. "Well, can you at least walk really far behind us? Like, where you can still see us?"

"Oh, I get it. You might see boys from school, and you don't want to be embarrassed by your dad hanging around. No problem. I'm a hip dude."

Grace looked at me, smiled, and rolled her eyes. "You've got us pegged, Dad," she said to him.

I loved the way Mr. Mills was strict but playful. It made me wonder how my relationship with my dad would be if he was still alive, and I was hit with a pang of envy.

The parking lot was almost completely full, so Mr. Mills parked far away from the door. He stood by his truck, letting us get a head start. I'd never seen so many people in one place before.

"Your shoe's untied," Grace said while we waited to cross.

I bent down and tied my shoe. When I stood, I saw her. She was sitting against the outside of the store about twenty feet to the side of the doors. It was my mom.

Grace grabbed my arm. "Come on, it's clear," she said, trying to pull me through the crosswalk. I didn't budge...I couldn't move.

"It's her," I said. "My mother."

Grace followed my gaze until she saw her. "Are you sure?" she asked.

"Yeah...I mean, I think so."

She was wearing cargo pants, a green shirt, and a black coat, all of which were about two or three sizes too big for her. Her hair was stringy and limp, and she looked dirty. This woman was not the same pretty young girl in the pictures with my father. For a second I thought maybe it wasn't her, but when she threw her head to the side to flip her hair from her eyes, I knew it was. She did that all the time when I was little.

"It is her. I think I'm going to puke," I said, as I turned around and started walking back to the truck. I was halfway there when Grace grabbed my arm and spun me around. Right there in the Walmart parking lot, she hugged me tight. Mr. Mills walked up.

"What's going on?"

Grace let go of me. "Erin's mother. Over there in the black coat."

Mr. Mills put his hand on my shoulder. "Do you want to come back another day, Erin?" he asked.

Grace looked at me.

"No, I'm okay. I just need a second."

A couple of people almost ran us down with their carts, so Mr. Mills suggested we go sit in the truck for a few minutes to regroup.

As we sat in the truck, I went over possible scenarios in my mind. What would I say to her? What would she say to me? Would she try to hug me? Would she tell me how much she'd missed me and ask how I'd been?

After a few minutes of sitting in silence, I took a deep breath. "I'm ready," I said, as I pulled the door handle.

"You sure?" Mr. Mills asked. "I don't mind bringing you girls back later."

"I'm sure."

I was trembling so hard, I was sure people could see my clothes vibrating. In the end though, I'd gotten worked up for nothing. As we got closer, my mom looked at Mr. Mills, then at me, and then Grace. Her eyes immediately darted back to me, and I held my breath.

For a few seconds, my mother gave me a puzzled look, as if she was seeing someone she thought she might know but couldn't quite place. Then, she looked away, and just like that, it was over, and we were in the store.

I turned to Grace. "She doesn't even know who I am. She doesn't even know HER OWN DAUGHTER!"

I felt the tears well up in my eyes. *Do NOT cry, Erin,* I told myself.

Grace grabbed my hand. "Come on, Erin. Let's find presents so we can get out of here." Then, turning to Mr. Mills, she said, "Remember to stay back."

"Got it," he answered.

It was hard to concentrate on shopping, but I tried my best. I knew if I let myself think about what had just happened, I might lose it right there in the store.

I ended up buying fleece throw blankets—a Redskins one for Pap and a light blue one with snowflakes for Gram. The lines were long, and while we waited, Grace was talking to me, but I couldn't focus on what she was saying.

I thought about confronting my mother. I'd go right up to her and ask her what kind of mother doesn't even recognize her own child. I also considered walking up to her and punching her in the face. By the time we got out of the store, she was gone. None of us spoke as we walked to the truck.

When we pulled out on the highway, Mr. Mills asked, "Are you all right, Erin?"

"Yeah."

"Do you want to come over and hang out at my house?" Grace asked.

"No, thanks."

I just wanted to be alone. None of us spoke the rest of the way home.

Chapter Thirteen

Mr. Mills pulled the truck into the driveway. I grabbed my bag. "Thanks, Mr. Mills."

"You're welcome, honey."

"Bye, Erin. Call me in a little while," Grace said.

"Okay."

I went inside, closed the door behind me as quietly as possible, and went straight to my room. I didn't feel like seeing or talking to Gram or Pap, and I hoped that they didn't know I'd come in. I locked my door, shoved the Walmart bag under my bed, and took my shoes off. Then I sat on my bed and cried.

I always believed that one day my mom would show up and tell me how much she missed me. She'd be drug-free. She'd tell me that she'd gotten a job and a place to stay, and that she wanted me to come live with her. Or maybe I just hoped that's what would happen. That hope had been squashed at Walmart. She wasn't drug-free, she wasn't coming to get me, and she obviously wasn't thinking about me. I was the last thing on her mind.

Gram knocked on my door.

"Erin, can I come in?"

I grabbed a dirty shirt off my floor, wiping my face off with it. I opened the door and sat back down on my bed.

"You've been crying. What's wrong?" Gram asked.

"I don't really want to talk about it."

"That's fine," Gram said, sitting down on the bed beside me.

We sat in silence for a few minutes. Gram put her arm around me, and suddenly I wanted to tell her.

"I saw my mom."

"What? Where?"

"She was at Walmart. Sitting out front."

"What did she say?"

"Nothing. She didn't know who I was." The words caught in my throat.

"Are you sure it was her?"

"Yeah."

Gram sighed. "Are you sure she saw you?"

"Yeah. She looked right at me."

"Erin, honey, I'm so sorry."

"You wanna know something funny, Gram? I remember every detail about the day she left. I remember sitting there on the front porch waiting. After a long time went by, I think I knew she wasn't coming back, so I started trying to figure out what I'd done to make her leave. The only thing I could come up with was the puppy."

"Puppy?"

"I wanted a puppy. I was obsessed, so I asked like, every week, at least. And every time I asked, she always said no, and I always argued about it. I just wanted one so bad. I had asked again that morning, and she got mad, so I thought maybe that's why she left."

Gram hugged me tight.

"Sweet, sweet girl. It breaks my heart that you thought it was your fault. Your momma is very sick, honey."

I was tired of hearing that my mom was sick.

"She's not sick, Gram. She's a junkie. She chose heroin over me. She left me sitting on that porch believing that I was so bad that my own mom couldn't stand to be around me anymore."

I had never cried about my mom in front of Gram or Pap before, and except for the one time with Grace, I'd kept it bottled up for years. Now, it was coming full force.

"I hate her!" I wiped the tears off my face with the back of my hand. "So, why am I upset? Why do I even care?"

"You care because she's your mom and you love her. Sometimes, we love people but at the same time, we don't like them. Erin, believe it or not, your mom does love you. I know it doesn't seem like it, but she does. She got mixed up with drugs, and drugs change people. She wasn't always the way she is now. She used to be a good mom."

"Gram, why did she start doing drugs?"

"I don't know, honey. I honestly don't know. She made a very stupid choice."

"I want you to tell me what happened. I'm not a little kid anymore. If you can't tell me why she started doing drugs, tell me when. Tell me something."

"I'll tell you what I know, but it's not much. After your father died, it was hard for every one of us, including your mom. For a while, she still came around, usually once or twice a week. She brought you with her. You were our only light during a very dark time. After a few months, she started coming around less often...maybe once, twice a month. I suspect that must have been about the time she started with the drugs, although we had no idea then."

Gram sighed and put her arm around me. She was quiet for a few seconds before she continued.

"Then one day, she stopped coming altogether. We called her, but she'd changed her number. We went to your house, but she'd moved. We asked neighbors, but no one knew anything. It was as if you both just disappeared into thin air. We even talked to the sheriff's office. We filed a missing person's report. They found y'all but said they couldn't tell us where you were. We thought that maybe your mom didn't want to be near us anymore; maybe seeing us reminded her of your dad, and it was too painful for her. As hard as it was, we decided to just be grateful that you were both alive and well...and hope that one day she'd change her mind. And we didn't hear anything else until the day after she left you. That's when the sheriff's office contacted us, and you came to live with us. That's all I know. And your mom is sick, Erin. I know it's not like cancer, but I honestly believe it is a disease...like a mental disorder, maybe."

"There's got to be more to it than that. Why did she start doing it? How could she be so stupid?" I was so frustrated I thought I was going to burst.

Gram shook her head. "I truly don't know. I think she probably thought she was just trying it and wouldn't get hooked. Maybe that's where the disease comes in; maybe addicts fool themselves. That'd be my guess."

Gram stood. "I'm going to go start dinner. You gonna be okay?"

"Yeah, I'm good," I said, forcing a tight smile. "Thanks, Gram."

Gram closed the door when she left. I'd never been open to the idea of talking about my mom to Gram or Pap. I thought talking to them would make me feel worse, but I actually felt better.

Chapter Fourteen

After dinner, I called Grace. She asked if I was okay, and I told her about my talk with Gram. I admitted that I'd always thought that my mom would get clean one day and come for me.

"I know it sounds stupid after what happened today, but I kind of still hope she will."

"I have a confession," Grace said. "Up until now, I was envious of you because even though she left you, she's still alive. I know my mom won't see me graduate. She won't see me get married or get to meet her grandkids. There's hope for you that your mom will be a part of all that. But after today, after seeing how torn up you were, I don't envy you as much. I hope you get your mom back, but not knowing and waiting around to find out must really suck."

"It does...let's change the subject."

"Okay. Whaddya wanna talk about?"

"Christmas. Let's talk about Christmas. I'm not getting a smartphone, but you might. We can use yours to practice calling boys. We can call each other Gram-style," I said.

"Perfect," she said. "I'll call you on your house phone, and when you answer, I'll hang up. Then you call me, and when I answer, you hang up. Then once we've got it down, we can call real, live guys and hang up on them."

"How will we get their phone numbers?" I asked. "I'm sure not asking George for his phone number."

"Chicken."

"Yep...a chicken with dignity."

"Chickens don't have dignity."

"The ones who don't ask for guys' phone numbers or call and hang up on them do."

"So," Grace said, "you'd rather be a dignified, lonely-for-the-rest-of-your-life chicken than an undignified, stalker-type girl with George's phone number. This is what you're telling me?"

"Of course."

We spent another ten minutes ranking farm animals by their level of dignity. Grace felt that the horse ranked highest on the dignity scale while I continued to argue for the chicken.

After we hung up, I showered and got in bed. I lay under my comforter looking up at the swirl patterns on the ceiling. Someone had spent hours making the same little swirls over and over until the whole ceiling was covered in swirls. *It must get boring,* I thought, *to spend day after day, in house after house, making swirls on ceilings.* Not only was it boring, it probably also gave the swirler horrible neck pain. That person, whoever he was, took care of his family by making those swirls day in and day out. That was a man who loved his wife, who loved his kids, and was willing to spend eight hours a day doing one of the most boring jobs on the planet to take care of his family. That guy wouldn't have left his five-year-old kid sitting on the front porch, but then again, most parents wouldn't.

Earlier, Grace had said that there was hope for my mom and me. She was right; there was hope, but very little of it. *It would be better if my mom would just die,* I thought. At least then, I'd have an ending. There would be some closure. I wouldn't ever have to worry about seeing her at Walmart or anywhere else for that matter. I wouldn't have to feel how I felt when I realized that she didn't know who I was. I wouldn't find myself loving her one minute, daydreaming about how wonderful things would be once she finally got clean, and then the next minute wishing she'd just overdose so I could forget about her once and for all. I thought I'd rather have all my hope taken away at once than have it taken away piece by piece.

"If you're gonna kill me, do it quick," is what the good guys in the movies would say.

Chapter Fifteen

There's always one Christmas in someone's life that they remember forever as their best Christmas. My first Christmas with Grace as my friend was my best Christmas. Her dad didn't have any brothers or sisters, and his parents lived in Florida and didn't like to travel. Her mom's parents also lived out of state and hadn't been to visit her and her dad since their daughter's funeral. At Christmas, it was usually just Grace and her dad. The thought of the two of them, without Grace's mom, made me feel sad for her, and I said so to Gram and Pap. The next time Mr. Mills dropped me off, Gram and Pap walked out to his truck.

"Hey there, Ed," Gram said.

"Hey, how's it going?"

"Going good," Gram said.

"Wanted to run something by ya," Pap said. "Since Grace and Erin have become so close and want to spend every minute together, we were hoping you would come over on Christmas day. We could watch the game and maybe drink a beer while the girls do their thing. Then, the wife's gonna feed us Christmas dinner. She's one helluva cook. Whaddya say?"

Mr. Mills just sat there for a few seconds, looking as if he was trying to think up an excuse why he couldn't come. Then he grinned, shrugged his shoulders and said, "Sure, why not."

Pap, looking quite pleased with himself, gave me a quick wink. He told Mr. Mills to come around noon.

I don't remember ever being really excited on Christmas Eve before. I don't even know if Santa came to visit me when I lived with my mom. After I moved in with Gram and Pap, even though I liked Christmas, it always made me sad because I missed my mom. I loved Gram and Pap, but it was just the three of us. This year was different; Grace and her dad would be spending the day with us.

There would be five of us sitting at the table for Christmas dinner. Gram said that Grace and I wouldn't be doing "our thing," like Pap had said, but that we would be helping her. That was fine by me. I liked the idea of the three of us working together to get dinner ready.

Ever since Gram helped us with our makeup, we liked having her around, as long as it wasn't for too long. We definitely didn't want her to overhear us talking about guys because someone who thinks it's a good idea to call and hang up on boys wasn't someone we wanted any relationship ideas or advice from.

I woke up a little after nine o'clock on Christmas morning. I heard someone rustling around in the kitchen, so I figured Gram was making breakfast. The rule was eat first, then open presents. Pap acted like if he did anything before breakfast, the result would be catastrophic like a heart attack or stroke, and Christmas was no exception.

After breakfast, we opened gifts. Gram and Pap loved their blankets. When they opened them, Pap asked me how I got the money to get them. I told him about the agreement that Grace and I had about how we'd spend our money. I think the fact that I bought gifts for them instead of my best friend touched them.

Every year, Gram and Pap gave me toys, underwear, socks, and some cute pajamas. This year, instead of toys, Gram changed things up by giving me makeup and one of those makeup mirrors that lights up. She also gave me a couple of bras, and I wished she'd waited until later to give me those. I could have melted into the floor opening them in front of Pap.

They had saved the big surprise for last. It was an iPhone!

"But I thought I couldn't have one!" I said.

Gram smiled. "Well, we talked about it some more and talked to Grace's dad, and he said he was getting Grace one. We decided to go ahead and get it. You need to understand, if you throw any more fits, or if your grades start to slip, the phone will be taken away indefinitely. Do you understand?"

"Yes, ma'am."

Gram had met Grace's dad at the phone store, and together they picked out both of our phones. Gram said they got us the exact same phones, but instead of a purple case like mine, they'd gotten Grace a blue one. I couldn't wait for Grace and her dad to get there.

Mr. Mills pulled into the driveway right at noon. I ran outside waving my phone over my head. "Look!"

Grace ran to me waving her phone over her head too, also yelling, "Look!"

Gram and Pap were waiting in the kitchen. Gram had started cooking, and Pap was sitting at the kitchen table drinking coffee and reading the paper. Pap got up and pulled out a chair. "Have a seat, Ed. Care for some coffee or a beer or something?"

"Coffee would be great, thanks."

Gram walked over to the cabinet for a coffee cup, then over to the coffee pot. Pap was always the one to ask if you needed or wanted something, and if you said yes, Gram was always the one who ended up getting it for you.

Gram poured the coffee into a coffee mug that had the words, "Jake's Auto Repare" written in red. Underneath, there was a drawing of a red car with Jake's phone number. Gram loved that mug, and every time she used it she said, "Sure hope Jake is better at fixing cars than he is at spelling!" Then, she'd laugh as if it was the first time that she'd ever told that joke.

I always wondered how many mugs Jake bought with that misspelling on it and why the company that made the mugs hadn't called him up before making them and asked him if he meant to spell it that way. If they had, Jake would have been saved a lot of embarrassment. Or maybe he'd told them over the phone what to write, and they had made the mistake. Either way, I felt kind of bad for Jake.

"Cream and sugar?" Gram asked.

"Just black, please."

Gram set the mug on the table in front of Mr. Mills. "Sure hope Jake is better at fixing cars than he is at spelling," Gram said, cackling.

"Pardon?"

Gram pointed to the word, "Repare" on the mug, and Mr. Mills said, "Oh!" and laughed too.

"We're going to my room," I told Gram. "Call us when you're ready for us to come help you."

"Okay, honey," Gram said.

We sat on my bed side-by-side with our new phones. The first thing we did was add each other to our contact list. After that, I added the only two other phone numbers I had—Grace's home phone number and my home number. After that, we took selfies of us together and made them our background photos for our phone home screens.

The real fun came when we downloaded the Instagram app. We searched for George and Good Jimmy and found them both. George's profile picture was a picture of him with what I assumed to be his family—a woman, a man, and a little boy. Since it wasn't a picture of him with a girl, I figured he didn't have a girlfriend. Jimmy's picture was just him. He used to date Bethany Foster, but they'd broken up. We guessed he didn't have a girlfriend, either.

Grace and I followed each other, but we didn't follow anyone else. We couldn't follow George and Jimmy (how obvious would that be?), and even though we didn't dislike the people at school, we didn't really know them well enough to follow them. I later learned that most of the kids at school actually like having a lot of followers even if they don't know them. I guess it makes them feel popular.

Grace found Jimmy Howes on there. He had over two hundred people following him, which was surprising since he was such a jerk. His profile picture was one that he had taken of himself shirtless while standing in front of his bathroom mirror. I thought that maybe he should save the shirtless pictures for when he could get his weight up over eighty pounds and grow some muscles. Better yet, he should've just kept all his clothes on because it seemed stupid for a guy to have a shirtless picture unless he was at the beach.

"I dare you to follow him," Grace teased.

"Are you crazy? You do it. I triple-dog dare you." We'd discovered the triple-dog dare from a Christmas movie we'd watched and thoroughly enjoyed using it, even though we never followed through.

"No way."

"Well, then I triple-dog dare you to follow Good Jimmy."

"Woman, you have lost your mind," Grace said.

"GIRLLLLS," Gram called, "I'm ready for you."

Gram didn't ask us to help cook because it was all pretty much done. Instead, she asked us to set the table and wash the dishes she'd messed up. She had timed everything perfectly. Once we had the dishes done, she had us set the food on the table. There was ham, turkey, mashed potatoes, gravy, candied yams with marshmallows (my favorite), green bean casserole, stuffing, and yeast rolls.

The finishing touch was the candle she'd placed in the middle of the table. She lit it and then called Mr. Mills and Pap to the table.

"Who wants to say the blessing?" Gram asked.

We all looked at each other, waiting for a volunteer. Pap finally spoke up. "I'll do it."

Gram grabbed my hand and I followed suit, grabbing Grace's hand. Once we were all holding hands, we bowed our heads, and Pap said, "Almighty Father, thank you for the wonderful food you've set before us. Thank you for the roof over our heads and all the other blessings that you've given us. Most of all, thank you for our health and for bringing us together as a family. And please, God, bless the brave men and women who serve our country. Amen."

We all echoed, "Amen," and then dug in.

Pap decided that Christmas dinner was the perfect time to lecture Grace and me. "Those new phones better not mess with your grades, girls."

We assured him that they wouldn't. Then Mr. Mills gave us a rundown on internet safety, reminding us that child predators are everywhere, and that human trafficking is very real. Normally, that type of lecturing would have elicited a secret eye roll between Grace and me, but we had seen so many bad things on the news that we knew he was right.

After we all finished eating, Grace and I had to give Mr. Mills our cell phones so that he could set parental controls on them. He showed Gram and Pap how everything worked. I didn't mind; I actually liked that he cared enough to worry about me. It made me feel like he considered me as family instead of just his daughter's friend.

We helped Gram clean up the dishes and put away the food. After Christmas dinner each year, Gram made hot chocolate. We would turn off the television and the lights, leaving the Christmas tree lit. Gram would turn the radio on to play Christmas music, and we would sit drinking our hot chocolate. It was a special thing we'd always done, and it was extra special this year with Grace and her dad there.

It was almost eight when they left. Grace texted me a few minutes after they'd gone and said that her dad told her what a nice time he'd had. I asked Gram and Pap if we could have them over again the next year, and they both agreed. They seemed to enjoy having the company. I hoped it was a tradition that would last forever.

That night, as I lay in bed looking at the swirls and thinking about what a perfect day it had been, I realized that I hadn't thought of my mom even once. For the first time in years, I hadn't felt sad on Christmas day. I wondered if she celebrated Christmas, but I doubted it. I could picture her in my mind...sitting in a dirty, roach-infested, dark, cold room in an abandoned house with no plumbing or electricity. She'd be wearing a coat, a hat, and gloves, only taking the coat and gloves off long enough to shoot up. I didn't know a whole lot about drug addicts, but I knew enough to know that any money they got their hands on probably didn't go towards rent or an electric bill. Her blonde hair would be hanging in greasy tendrils around her face. She wouldn't have eaten in a day or more, but she wouldn't care because nothing, nothing at all, but the next fix mattered.

Suddenly, I felt horrible for what I had wished a few weeks ago. I remembered what Gram said—that she had been a good mom before the drugs. I thought about the fact that she didn't have any family around and how alone and scared she must have been when my dad died. And then my mind went back to her alone in that cold, dark room. Maybe other people were there, but if they were, they were just there to do drugs.

That's when I had another realization. I'd always thought about my mom in regard to how I felt, how hurt I was, how horrible it was that she left me. Never once, until now, had I thought about what it must feel like to be her.

Yes, she'd made stupid, selfish choices, but those choices were hurting her so much more than they hurt me. I'd spent Christmas in a warm house with people who loved me, while she spent her Christmas in the lonely underworld of drugs. I wasn't excusing what she did to me or to herself, but for the very first time, I wasn't thinking about how I was affected by her drug use; I was thinking about how she was affected by it.

Every bit of anger completely left me, and I was left with only sorrow and sympathy. I looked at the clock; it was 11:03 p.m. I had almost made it through Christmas day without being sad, but this time when the sadness came, it was different...this time, I wasn't sad for myself.

Chapter Sixteen

Usually, Christmas break flies by, and before you know it, you're standing at the bus stop freezing your butt off, impatiently waiting for that heated, yellow bus to show up and take you to the last place on earth you want to go. This year was different. I was excited to go back to school. Honestly, I was only excited about two classes—English, because I liked that class, and science, because I liked George.

There was a dance coming up in a couple of weeks, and I hoped he was going but I didn't want to come out and ask him if he was. It turned out that I didn't have to worry about it because Angie Blake took care of it for me.

Angie Blake was one of the most popular girls in school. She was definitely one of the prettiest, with her long, dark hair and her perfect body and face. She knew how pretty she was, and she practically demanded special treatment because of it. In most cases, she didn't have to make any demands, but in the rare case that a boy wasn't drooling over her, she went out of her way to change that.

I liked a lot about George, but one thing I really liked was the fact that he didn't pay any attention at all to

Angie Blake, which drove her completely nuts. She sat on the other side of him and was worse than a little kid in a toy store tugging at her mother's skirt. "Geooorge, can you help me with the assignment?"

"Geooorge, what's today's date?"

"How was your weekend, Geooorge?"

The fact that she couldn't say his name without drawing it out for a year was annoying enough, but even worse was that she obviously already knew the answer to her questions and just asked as an excuse to get his attention, which she didn't get much of, anyway. He usually gave her a one-word reply in an irritated tone. Sometimes he would turn to me and roll his eyes.

In this instance though, I could have kissed her. We had been back from the holiday break for a couple of days. It was near the end of class. "Geooorge, are you going to the dance?"

I pretended to keep working on my assignment, acting like I hadn't heard the question.

"Yeah," George said.

I started packing up my stuff as I tried not to smile.

"Do you dance? If so, save me a slow one," she said.

"No can do," George replied. "I'm going to the dance with Erin."

My heart jumped, and I turned to him.

"What?" Angie and I asked simultaneously.

George looked at me and winked. "Yep, going with Erin," he said, as the bell rang.

I knew the wink meant that he wasn't serious and wanted me to play along, and this time, my heart sunk.

"Oh, okay. Didn't know you two were a thing. Sorry, Erin," she said as she grabbed her book bag and walked out.

"Yeah, neither did I," I said, speaking to George. "Thanks for using me as your get-out-of-Angie-card." I felt the tears start to well up. What a crappy thing to do.

"Wait, Erin," he said as I headed for the door. "Wait."

I stopped but I didn't look at him; I didn't want him to see the tears. He got in front of me.

"Wow, you're really upset. I'm sorry. And I wasn't using you for anything. I was planning to ask you if you wanted to hang out at the dance. I just hadn't yet, and then Angie kind of forced my hand."

"Oh," I said with a shrug, trying to downplay my initial reaction.

"I'm sorry. I didn't mean to make you mad. No more surprises, I promise."

He had planned on asking me after all!

"Swear it?" I asked.

"Swear it," he said, and then promptly knocked me down from cloud nine again with, "You're one of my buds. I'd never piss you off on purpose."

That afternoon, I called Grace as soon as I got home and told her the whole story.

"Guys suck," was her reply.

"George doesn't suck; he just doesn't like me as anything more than a friend. So, not all guys suck. Good Jimmy doesn't suck, so there's two out of millions that are okay."

"Actually, Good Jimmy does suck. Good Jimmy is no longer Good Jimmy...he's Sucky Jimmy."

"What happened?" I asked.

Grace was right; Sucky Jimmy was an appropriate name for Jimmy Steiner. Devin, one of the boys in Grace and Jimmy's gym class, was deaf. Not completely deaf, but deaf enough that it affected his speech. Apparently, Sucky Jimmy thought that making fun of the way Devin spoke would be a great way to entertain Jimmy's band of friends.

"So, he's standing there, right in Devin's face, with William Jacobs and Logan Crawford standing around him, and he starts imitating the way Devin talks. But he doesn't just imitate, he talks really loud and is totally, one hundred percent exaggerating how Devin sounds. Then, to top it off, he starts crossing his eyes and letting his tongue hang out of his mouth. William and Logan are laughing their butts off, but nobody else was. Erin, it was so bad. You could see that poor Devin was about to cry. I started to go tell Jimmy to cut it out but before I could get there, WHAM! Devin punched him right in the nose and broke it! It was the best thing I've ever seen in my life! So, anyway, I'm not into Jimmy anymore."

"Wow. I can't believe that Jimmy would act that way. I would have never pegged him as a bully. It's awesome that Devin broke his nose."

"Yeah, everyone thought it was great. I should've known Jimmy was a jerk," Grace said. "He hunts."

"Huh?"

"Yeah, I was talking to him the other day, and he said that he and his dad shot a deer over holiday break. A deer, Erin. Not a bear or some other animal that goes around killing people, but a poor, defenseless deer. I kind of didn't like him anymore then, anyway. The thought of people killing for sport makes me sick. Plus, what if we got together, stayed together, got married, and had kids? Huh? I guess he'd teach my sons the fine sport of killing innocent animals? I don't think so."

I laughed. "Married? Are you serious? I mean, I know you're a planner, but—"

"Dead serious...no pun intended."

Chapter Seventeen

When George informed me that he considered me just a friend, I'd been bummed, but that same night, as I lay in bed looking at the swirls and thinking, it hit me that when Angie had referred to us as a thing, George hadn't corrected her. He may have thought of me as only a friend, but he didn't mind if Angie thought we were more.

It was probably wishful thinking to believe that maybe he liked me as a girlfriend. At the very least, he wasn't ashamed for people to think he liked me as more than a friend, and possibly he felt the same way about me as I did about him. I needed to be patient, and even if he never liked me like a girlfriend, at least I would still be able to see him in class every day for the rest of the school year.

But what about when school let out? What if we didn't have any classes together the next year? I panicked and grabbed my phone, got on Instagram, and sent him a request to follow him. I didn't have to worry about it being awkward, because if we were "buds" in school, we could be "buds" on Instagram too.

Within a minute, he had accepted my request. A second later, I received a request from him to follow me! It was almost midnight, so after taking a quick peek at his pictures, I put the phone back on my nightstand and looked up at the swirls again, wondering why he was still awake. Did he have swirls on his ceiling also? If so, did he stare at them to think, like I did? I let myself think that if he did, he sometimes thought about me.

The weeks leading up to the dance went by slowly. The theme of the dance was "A New Hope," thanks to the fact that the planning committee for the dance consisted of a bunch of *Star Wars* fanatics.

The day of the dance finally came. During class, George told me he'd be there around seven. Grace and I had our plan all worked out. The dance started at sixty thirty and lasted until nine thirty. Pap and Gram would drive me, and we'd pick Grace up from her house at six fifteen, so we'd be there right on time. I planned on spending the night at Grace's house, so Mr. Mills would be picking us up from the dance.

During science class, George said, "Give me your number, and I'll text you when I get there."

"Okay. It's...six, four, zero-umm, six, four, zero," I stammered. Suddenly, I had no idea what my own phone number was.

George shook his head. "Give me your phone, blondie."

I handed him my phone and said a silent prayer that he wouldn't see any clues on it that would alert him to the fact that I was pretty much obsessed with him.

Knowing my luck, this would be the exact moment that Grace would send me a text saying something like, "Getting excited for your big date with Prince George?" Luckily, that didn't happen.

He handed my phone back. "I put my number in your contacts, so send me a text now, and I'll have your number."

I typed "GEORGE" in contacts, but nothing came up. "I'm typing your name, but you aren't coming up," I said.

"That's because I put my alias in there. Type in, 'The Incredibly Good-Looking and Talented George Barnes.'"

My first text to The Incredibly Good-Looking and Talented George Barnes was, "SERIOUSLY?" followed by the eye-rolling emoji. I think he liked that.

I couldn't eat dinner that night. I was too excited. Even though Gram had taught me how to put on makeup, I hadn't done it enough to get the hang of it, so I asked her to do it for me.

"You never wear makeup. You must have your sights on some boy." She patted the bed. "Sit right here. Who is this special boy?"

"Nobody, Gram."

"Now, I know better than that. Come on. Out with it. What's his name?"

I knew she wouldn't give up. "His name is George, but he's just a friend."

"Hmm...," she said. "Look down."

I tried not to move as she put the eyeliner on my lids. It tickled.

"Look up. What's he look like?"

"Just regular, I guess," I said as she put my mascara on.

"Just regular, huh? Well, I'm sure that when just-regular-George sees you, he's going to be smitten."

"I doubt it. He sees me all the time in class and he's not smitten, so I don't see how a little bit of makeup is gonna change that. This isn't a Disney movie, you know."

Gram chuckled. "I know. But this also isn't class. It's a dance. Just as much magic can happen at a dance as it does in a Disney movie."

"Well, hopefully Mr. Mills's truck won't turn into a pumpkin on the way to pick us up. That would be embarrassing."

Gram laughed. "You're funny. All done," she said. "We'll be in the living room whenever you're ready to leave."

I looked in the mirror. I didn't look half bad. I wasn't Angie Blake, that's for sure, but I wasn't hideous either. I put on a blue cami under a white, off-the-shoulder top with my jeans and looked in the mirror at the finished product. Definitely not Disney. Not even close.

Chapter Eighteen

We got to Grace's house, and she came out wearing jeans too. I wished that Good Jimmy had stayed good until after the dance. I wanted to spend time alone with George but that wasn't going to happen now that Grace didn't have Jimmy to distract her. I knew it was selfish and I felt bad; after all, she was my best friend, but this was also the only chance I had to be around George outside of class. I hoped a cute, nice guy would come and talk to Grace. That way, we'd both have a great time, and I wouldn't feel guilty.

The lady at the door took our money and gave us tickets. "Have a good time, ladies," she said. We thanked her and headed for the gym.

It looked amazing. I was expecting it to be adorned with a bunch of ugly spaceships and even uglier aliens, but instead, it looked beautiful. Tiny lights that were supposed to be stars blanketed the ceiling, and two huge moons hung on a backdrop that covered one whole wall of the gym. George later informed me that the two moons were, in fact, not moons but setting suns. Sparkly paper stars dangled from the rafters. Gram was right; it was magical.

I was relieved to see that my classmates were also wearing the same types of clothes they wore to school every day. I figured that dressing up must not be a thing until the ring dance and homecoming, so I had plenty of time to gear myself up for something fancier.

We walked around the perimeter of the gym until we came to the DJ. He was forty-something, balding, and looked like he smoked too many cigarettes and ate too much fast food. He had a table set up with a sign hanging from it that said, "JD'S DJ SERVICE—WEDDINGS, GRADUATIONS, AND ALL SPECIAL OCCASIONS."

I looked at Grace. "JD the DJ?"

"I know, right?" she said, laughing.

There were some kids standing around his table and one asked, "Do you take requests?"

"Sure thing, kiddo, as long as it's clean. Don't be askin' for me to play no Lil Wayne up in here," JD the DJ said, and then laughed the way that Gram always laughed about the misspelled mug.

"Look who just walked up," Grace whispered.

It was Bad Jimmy. I wondered if we could just go back to calling him Jimmy now that Good Jimmy was Sucky Jimmy and wouldn't be a part of our conversations anymore.

Of course, he noticed us right away.

"Looking fine tonight, ladies," he said, giving Grace the once-over. Then, he gave me the once-over and said to Grace, "Well, one of you, anyway."

I acted like I didn't hear him.

"Erin's wearing makeup. Who you tryin' to look good for?" he asked.

"Shut up," Grace said as she grabbed my arm and started walking in the other direction. "Don't pay attention to him, Erin. There's something seriously wrong with him."

"Thanks. Out of all the people in this school, I don't know why he decided to pick on me. From the very first day, remember?"

"How could I forget?" she asked. "I remember thinking that he must be blind, because I thought you were really pretty. Oh my God, that's it! He doesn't think you're ugly at all! Jimmy Howes has a crush on you!"

"Yeah, right. That's why he calls me ugly every chance he gets."

"He does that because he doesn't want you to know that he has the hots for you, dummy."

I thought about it but doubted he could like anybody. He was a jerk, so even though I'd never seen him pick on anyone else, that didn't tell me much. We only had one class together. For all I knew, he found one unlucky victim to torture in each of his classes.

"I doubt it, but if you're right, I guess I'm just lucky," I said.

"Lucky, huh?" asked a familiar voice from behind me.

It was George. He was with Scott Adams, who was in my math class. Scott was a nice guy.

"Hey, Erin. Hey, Grace." Scott said.

"Hey, Scott. Did you come together?" I asked.

"Yeah, but we're not a couple," George said, looking at me. "We aren't a thing."

For the rest of the evening, the four of us just stood around and talked. Scott and Grace danced a few times, but George didn't ask me to dance. That was a relief because I didn't know how to dance and if I'd said no, he would have thought I didn't like him, but if I said yes, I would have had to make an idiot of myself in front of him.

Thankfully, Jimmy Howes didn't come around anymore, but Angie made sure to stop and say hello to George. Of course, she looked great. I thought about how funny it would be if she and Jimmy Howes got together, but that would never happen. Angie would never give him the time of day.

The highlight of the evening for me was when Scott said something to George, and he busted out laughing. There was something about that laugh. It was big, and happy, and full of everything lovely. It would make even the grouchiest person smile. I imagined how nice it must be to live in the same house with him. His family got to hear that laugh all the time.

"Hey, how come you don't have a profile picture?" George asked.

"I haven't had Instagram very long. Plus, I don't have any good pictures of myself," I said.

"Well, let's get one of you and me. Anyone standing next to me is gonna look good," he said, grinning.

With that, he grabbed his phone, put his arm around my shoulder and pulled me close. He held his cell phone up and snapped a picture.

He looked at the picture. "Not bad. I'll text it to you. You can crop me out of it if you want to, but then you run the risk of the picture not looking as good."

"Vain, much?" I asked.

That was the next best thing I liked about George. He wasn't conceited at all, but as a joke, he pretended to be. My phone vibrated. There it was, a text from "The Incredibly Good-looking and Talented George Barnes." He was right; it was a good picture of us. We weren't a couple, and I wasn't about to crop him out, so while I wouldn't be using it for a profile picture, I knew I'd probably look at it a thousand times. When Scott and Grace finished dancing, we took some selfies with us together. One of those would definitely be my profile picture.

"My dad just texted. He's here. We gotta go," Grace said.

I looked at my phone. It was already 9:25 p.m.

George gave me a hug. "See ya Monday."

"Yep, see ya."

While we were riding to Grace's, I pulled my phone out and looked at the photos George had sent. I showed Grace the one with all four of us that I liked best.

"This one's gonna be my profile picture," I said.

"Mine too," she said.

Mr. Mills asked us if we had a good time, and we gave him the eh-it-was-okay routine.

Once we were in the privacy of Grace's bedroom though, there were no "ehs" to be found.

"Scott is pretty awesome," Grace said. "He's cute too. Horrible dancer, but cute."

"Yeah, I like Scott. And there's nothing wrong with bad dancing, thank you." I was glad that George had brought him and especially glad that Grace had fun hanging out with him.

"So, did I miss anything with George? Did he try to hold your hand? Did he say anything about dating?"

"Nope, he was the same way he always is," I said.

I looked at the photo of the two of us.

"Somebody's got it bad," Grace said.

"I was just finding the other pictures so that I can put up a profile picture," I said.

"Mmm-hmmm."

Grace knew. She was the only person on the planet who knew that I liked George as more than a friend. But even she didn't know just how much I liked him, especially after the dance. Being around him was better than being around anyone, and as soon as we left the dance, I wished I could rewind the night and start it all over, beginning with the moment he walked up behind me. Was this what love felt like? And how old do you have to be to be in love?

Chapter Nineteen

My birthday is February 13. I was born at 10:59 p.m. If my mom had held out for sixty-one more minutes, I would have been born on Valentine's Day. Thank God she didn't.

Every year, we did the same thing for my birthday. Gram made me whatever I wanted for dinner and my favorite strawberry cake. I usually got whatever toy (or clothes and books when I got older) I'd been eyeing, as long as it didn't cost more than fifty bucks.

Gram and Pap said that fifty bucks was pushing it for a kid's birthday present and that any parent who went over that amount shouldn't be allowed to raise children. I'd never had a birthday party, but I didn't mind because Gram and Pap used the money they would have spent on a party towards my present.

"You can't have a big party and an expensive present. That's what's wrong with kids nowadays," Pap would say. "Their parents give 'em everything they ask for, and when they grow up, they expect the same from everyone, everywhere. It's asinine if you ask me."

This year, I didn't know what I wanted. I was too old for toys, and I didn't want clothes. Gram kept asking me what I wanted for my birthday, but I couldn't think of anything.

"Well, you need to think of something soon, otherwise, you'll be opening a big box of nothing come February thirteenth," she said.

Then, that Sunday, a week before the big day, it hit me. Gram was in the kitchen fixing dinner.

"I figured out what I want for my birthday," I announced.

"Oh good. What?"

"I want three friends over for pizza and movies on Saturday, since it's the night before my birthday."

"It's okay with me if it's okay with Pap...wait, what friends?"

"Grace, George, and Scott."

"Ohhhh," Gram said, smiling. "Okay. Well, go ask Pap. Tell him I'm okay with it."

Pap was sitting in his recliner watching a western. "Pap, Gram said it would be okay with her if I have some friends over for pizza and movies on Saturday for my birthday. She said to see if it's okay with you. Is it?"

"Sure thing," Pap said. And that was that.

"Thanks, Pap." I told Gram that Pap said it was okay, ran to my room, and sent Grace a text telling her my plan.

"YESSS!" she replied.

After dinner, I sat on my bed looking at my phone. I needed to text George and invite him, and ask him to invite Scott, but I couldn't think of how to ask without coming across either too casual or too excited.

Oh, good grief, Erin, I told myself, *just text the stupid invite.*

So, I did. I made it sound like it was already a plan to have Grace over for pizza and a movie and that he and Scott could come too if they wanted. I didn't tell him it was for my birthday. I didn't want him to think that I expected a present.

He didn't answer right away. In fact, he didn't answer until almost an hour later. "I'll be there. And I'll let Scott know. What time?"

I told him six although I hadn't even thought about that yet.

It was going to be a very long week, even longer than the stretch before the dance. That night, when I was in bed, I didn't look at the swirls. Instead, I looked at the picture...the one of George and me. I remembered his laugh and decided that at least one of the two movies we'd watch on Saturday would be funny—really funny. I thought about how happy I felt and realized how lucky I was to have such great friends.

It had been a month since I'd thought about my mom. I mean *really* thought about her, not just a passing thought. Was I not thinking about her because George consumed all my thoughts? If so, that was the third best thing I liked about him. Thinking about my mom always, without fail, made me sad or angry, so it felt good to not think about her. Yet, here I was thinking about her now. *Well, that's an easy fix,* I thought, as I switched my brain back to thoughts of George.

The next day in English class, Mr. Thompson gave us the details of our big assignment. "Every week, you've made up a new character, and you've written about that character. Now, the fun starts. I want you to take two or three of your favorite characters and write a story to include all of them. I'd like for the story to be at least ten pages, double-spaced. If you want it to be longer, that's fine. You've got a month to work on this, so ten pages isn't too much to ask. If you need help at any time during this process, come see me. I won't write it for you, but I can help with the mechanics of it."

A few of my classmates moaned. "What if we didn't keep those assignments after you handed them back?" Jimmy Howes asked.

"He told us every single week that we had to keep them," Grace said.

"Thank you, Grace. Jimmy, she's right. I guess you'll have to work from memory."

"I didn't say I didn't keep them. I asked what if," Jimmy said, smirking.

Mr. Thompson sighed. I wondered how many times a day he regretted becoming a teacher. Day in, day out, year after year, a kid like Jimmy in every class. Mr. Thompson probably looked forward to the end of the school year as much as we did.

I wouldn't have admitted it, but I was excited to write my story. I already had an idea of what I wanted it to be about, and I also knew which of my characters I'd use. I raised my hand.

"Yes, Erin?" Mr. Thompson said, looking relieved, probably because he knew I wouldn't ask a typical Jimmy Howes question.

"Can we use more than three characters?"

"Sure. But if you do, make them more background characters. Give them a small part. Does that make sense?"

I nodded my head. I'd read enough stories and watched enough movies to know that some characters only had a few lines, and some didn't even have any lines at all.

When I got home that day, I went straight to my room and started writing. It was harder than I thought it would be, but once I got into it, the words seemed to appear on their own. By dinner, I had three pages written. I read them over and felt that my story was pretty good so far. I decided I'd work on it some more the next day since I had other homework to do after dinner.

By Friday, the story was done. I was glad Mr. Thompson said we could go over ten pages because it ended up being fifteen pages long. It was hard to tell a whole story in just ten pages. Also, it gave me something to concentrate on while I waited for Saturday to arrive.

Chapter Twenty

On Saturday morning during breakfast, Gram got up and went into the living room. She came back with a square package, wrapped in multicolored paper that said "HAPPY BIRTHDAY" all over it, and set it on the table beside me.

"We wanted you to have something to open. Go on, open it," she said.

"My birthday isn't until tomorrow though."

"Oh, it's just a little something. You may want to use it before tomorrow."

I tore the paper off, crumpled it up, and threw it in the trash can. Gram had put my gift in a plain, cardboard box and had sealed the box with packing tape. Pap came over with the little pocketknife he always carried in his pocket, which came in handy more often than you'd think, and cut across the tape. Inside the box were goodies from the Bath & Body Works store in the mall: lotion, body wash, and body spray—all Warm Vanilla Sugar scented. I took the cap off the body spray and smelled it.

"Thanks! It smells delicious."

Gram smiled. "I thought you might like it," she said. "Put a small spray on your wrist and rub your wrists together. Perfume goes on your pulse points."

Pap smiled and rolled his eyes. "Reminds me of the hunters using deer urine to attract deer."

"Oh, hush!" Gram said and winked at me. She was right. I did like it, and I would be using it before the next day. I had never used any perfume before because it reminded me of old ladies and gave me a headache, but the night was going to be special. And besides, this scent didn't smell like old ladies or headaches—it smelled like cookies baking.

After breakfast, I went to my room and pulled out my story. I read it over, making corrections and changes with a pen. Once that was done, I went on Instagram. I had more than fifty people I was following and who followed me; they were all kids from school. Some of them posted funny pictures and videos, some posted inspiring photos and memes, and one or two (including Angie) posted at least one selfie every single day.

I'd once read an article that said people who post tons of selfies probably have low self-esteem. I couldn't imagine why anyone who looked like Angie would have low self-esteem.

None of this made much time pass, so I went back into the kitchen where Gram was pouring coffee for her and Pap. I followed her into the living room. Pap was watching another old western movie. Gram handed him his coffee, and I realized I'd completely forgotten to pick out movies to watch.

"Gram, what movies should we watch tonight?"

Gram and Pap had a large collection of DVDs. Some, mostly Disney, had been purchased over the years for me, but those were kids' movies, so they were a no-go.

"Let's see," Gram said as she walked over to the DVD cabinet. "What kind of movies are you looking for?"

"No Disney or kid movies. Something of yours and Pap's. I think funny movies would be best."

"Well, there's tons of those to choose from. We are clowns, after all, so funny is our thing."

Gram tilted her head sideways and ran her index finger over the titles, vetoing certain ones as she went along and pulling out ones she felt were a maybe.

Together, we decided on *50 First Dates*, which Pap said was cute, and *Dumb and Dumber*, which he said was his all-time favorite. I didn't completely trust their judgment, seeing as how they were two generations ahead of me.

"Are you sure these are funny? They're not babyish or for really old people, right?" I asked.

Gram shot a funny look my way.

"They're good movies," Pap said. "And if they turn out to be flops, Gram and I can always juggle for you."

I imagined how mortifying that would be. "No, that's okay, Pap. These movies are probably fine. Um...are y'all going to be hanging out in here with us?" I asked. I was hoping they would go watch television in their room. Not that I thought we'd be doing anything wrong; it would just be awkward to have my grandparents around.

"We won't be in here cramping your style, but we will be nearby, in the kitchen," Gram said. She must have seen the look on my face because she added, "I promise, you won't even notice we're here. We may be old, but we can definitely find something to occupy ourselves with. We haven't played cards in a long time. Bob, think you're up for a couple of games of Hand and Foot?"

"Sure. We can even spice things up a little. Let's throw some cash into it."

"You're on," Gram said.

Chapter Twenty-One

I had showered with my new body wash and put on the lotion and spray. I was careful not to use too much of either. Grace came at five thirty, and for the next thirty minutes, we drove Gram nuts.

Six o'clock finally arrived. "Stop running back and forth to the window. You girls are going to wear a hole in the floor," Gram said.

At 6:05, a minivan pulled into the driveway. Grace and I ran from the window, squealing like two little kids. I opened the front door, trying to look nonchalant as George, Scott, and a very tall, brown-haired man walked up.

"Hey, come on in," I said.

Pap reached out and shook the tall man's hand. "Bob Whitaker, good to meet ya. This is my wife, Trish." Then, the tall man shook Gram's hand.

"Nice to meet you both. I'm Eli Barnes, George's dad." I could see the resemblance.

"Hi, Mr. Barnes. I'm Erin. This is my friend, Grace. Gram, Pap, this is George, and this is Scott."

We went into the living room while the adults talked. Gram told Mr. Barnes that eleven o'clock would be a good time to pick up George and Scott. I grabbed the two movies we'd picked out.

"Have y'all seen these?" None of them had seen either movie. "Gram says they're both good, but Pap said *Dumb and Dumber* is hilarious."

"They're your grandparents?" George asked.

I hadn't even thought about telling him I lived with my grandparents, so now I'd lay it all out briefly and then change the subject as quickly as possible.

"Yeah, they're my dad's mom and dad. My dad died when I was two, and my mom left when I was five, so I've lived with them ever since. What kind of pizza do you want?" I was hoping he wouldn't ask any more questions, and he didn't.

"I've got a cousin whose friend went to live with his grandparents last year because his parents are junkies. I like pepperoni," George said. "Scott, pepperoni, right?"

Scott nodded.

Right then, Gram and Pap came in. "We're getting ready to order the pizzas. What kind do y'all want?" Gram asked.

"George and Scott like pepperoni. Grace and I want cheese."

We decided we'd eat before starting the movies. While we waited for the pizza, we sat in the living room talking. Scott sat in Pap's recliner, and Grace sat in the other recliner, so that left the couch for George and me—we sat on opposite ends.

I was afraid it would be awkward, but luckily Scott was outgoing and kept the conversation flowing. We talked about the school gossip and somehow Jimmy Howes came up.

"Oh, he's got it bad for Erin," Grace said. I shot her a look, but it was too late.

"Jimmy Howes, huh?" George said. "I would never guess to put you two together."

"He never said that. Grace thinks he likes me because he picks at me. I can't stand him."

"Nobody can," Scott said. "I used to be friends with him until seventh grade. He was actually okay before then, so I don't know what happened. Maybe his parents' divorce messed him up."

"That's no excuse," I snapped. "Lots of people have bad things happen to them, and they don't magically change into complete jerks."

Nobody said anything. They all just sat there staring.

"Sorry. Didn't mean to get worked up about it. I just don't think people should be given a pass to be jerks, that's all," I said.

"Not unless they're incredibly talented and good-looking like me," George said. "Oh, and I left out intelligent. I'm also very intelligent, in case you hadn't noticed."

I wanted to hug George. I'd gone on a mini-rant, and instead of running to the nearest exit, he'd made light of the situation.

"Yes," I said. "You are."

When the pizzas came, Gram and Pap took theirs in the living room, and the four of us sat at the kitchen table eating. I thought five large pizzas were a bit much until I saw how much George and Scott could eat. Between the two of them, they ate almost two whole pizzas. Everything was going fine until we finished eating. That's when Gram came in with my birthday cake. "HAPPY BIRTHDAY, ERIN!" it said, along with two candles—a one and a five.

"It's your birthday?" George asked.

"Tomorrow." I looked at Gram. I think she knew I was embarrassed. "But I didn't think we were celebrating tonight. We are definitely not singing, right, Gram?" I gave her a look, and she knew exactly what I was trying to say.

"No, no birthday singing," she said, lighting the candles. "But you do have to make a wish and blow the candles out."

I closed my eyes and blew. Since there were only the two candles, they weren't hard to blow out. While Gram cut the cake, I realized this was another first. This was the first time that my wish hadn't been about my mom. This year, it had been about George.

"Happy birthday, Erin," George said.

"Yeah, happy birthday," Scott said.

"Good cake, Mrs. Whitaker," George said. "Strawberry's my favorite." I didn't feel embarrassed anymore.

We watched *50 First Dates* first. Pap was right; it was cute, but not hilarious. When it was over, we all ate a second helping of cake. Afterwards, I sat back down on the couch, and this time, George sat right beside me. "You smell good," he said, "like cookies."

"Thanks."

Pap was also right about *Dumb and Dumber*. During some parts, we laughed until we had tears streaming down our faces. The whole movie was funny, so George laughed a lot. About halfway through the movie, George took my hand. He was holding my hand!

"Is this okay?" he asked.

I wanted to say something romantic, like, "It's perfect. You're perfect," but I couldn't speak so I just smiled and nodded. Later, I was glad I hadn't been able to speak because what I thought seemed romantic at the time, would have been cheesy and stupid. Sometimes, social anxiety can work in your favor.

We held hands throughout the rest of the movie. Grace and Scott stayed put in their recliners, but they talked and joked with each other a lot. A couple of times, I tried to sneak glances at George. Both times he caught me and smiled.

Eleven o'clock came fast, and George's dad pulled up right on time. We walked George and Scott to the door. Gram and Pap didn't follow. George gave me a hug. "See you Monday, but you can text me before then...if you want to," he said.

"Okay."

After George and Scott left, I found myself replaying the whole night, especially the part when George held my hand. Up until that moment, I never would have considered handholding to be a big deal, but with George being the one to hold my hand, it was a huge deal.

"Gram, tonight was great. Thanks so much for everything," I said, as we helped clean up the kitchen.

"Yeah, thanks, Mrs. Whitaker," Grace said.

"You're very welcome. I'm glad you had a nice time. Your friends seem like nice boys."

"They are," I said. It was sweet of Gram and Pap to stay in the kitchen. Pap had only come into the living room one time and that was to get his reading glasses. Gram hadn't come in at all. "Thanks for not hovering, Gram."

Gram chuckled. "You think I came out of the birth canal as an old person, don't you? I was your age once. And believe it or not, I liked boys too."

"I know. You liked to call them and hang up on them," I said.

"We didn't always hang up...only when we lost our nerve. We didn't call boys for the purpose of hanging up on them."

"Well, our generation has texting," Grace said. "If you write a text, you'd better make sure you really want to send it because once you hit the send button, it's gone and you ain't gettin' it back, Jack."

Gram laughed.

"Now, once you've texted a lot," Grace continued with a bad imitation of a deep-south accent, "then you can call, but us youngins' prefer to text. Look at this face," she said, crossing her eyes at Gram. "This is the face of modern technology and the future of 'Murica, Mrs. Whitaker."

"You girls are a mess! And it's midnight, so go on to bed so you don't sleep until noon tomorrow."

We said our goodnights to her and Pap and got ready for bed.

Once we were under the covers, I turned to face Grace. "Let's talk."

"For a minute," she said. "I'm pretty tired."

"I had so much fun tonight. Did you?"

"I did. George and Scott are pretty fun. And I saw y'all holding hands. He really likes you. I can tell." She thought for a moment and then said, "I wish Good Jimmy wouldn't have ended up being Sucky Jimmy."

"You don't like Scott?"

"Sure, he's nice. But I liked Jimmy a lot. Also, Scott may not like me like that, and even if he did, I don't know if I like him like that. But I do have fun when we all hang out."

"Me too," I said. "Hey, Grace?"

"Yeah?"

"Thanks for being the best friend in the world."

"You don't have to thank me. I love you," she said and rolled over. "Now go to sleep, weirdo. I'm tired."

It took me a while to fall asleep because I couldn't stop thinking about how good it felt when George held my hand and how I didn't want to let go when he'd hugged me.

Chapter Twenty-Two

At nine thirty, the house phone rang, waking me up. After a few seconds, I remembered what a great night I'd had, and I was instantly grinning. I sat up and looked over at Grace. She had her mouth wide open, snoring. Even after I got up, got dressed, brushed my teeth, and washed my face, Grace was still asleep. It was after ten o'clock when we finally got to the kitchen, but Gram and Pap weren't there. I walked into the living room. Gram was saying something to Pap, but when she saw me come in, she stood and told him, "We'll finish this later." They both wished me a happy birthday.

"Who wants birthday pancakes?" she asked.

"We do, of course," Grace said.

"Grace, what time is your dad picking you up?"

"Eleven. I'll go get my stuff." Grace went to my room and came back out with her plastic shopping bag. She always used a plastic grocery store bag to bring her pajamas over, but she had a toothbrush that stayed at our house.

We had just finished eating when Grace's dad pulled up. When she was gone, I started to clean off the table. "No, sit," Gram said. "Pap and I want to talk to you."

Uh-oh, I thought. *Pap saw me holding George's hand last night. They're gonna give me 'the talk.'* I already knew about all that stuff. Everyone my age knows, and half of them are already doing it, so I never understood why parents wait until after their kids are older than ten or eleven to have 'the talk.'

Pap looked at Gram and she looked at him, neither of them saying anything. Then Gram turned to me. "Erin, your mother called this morning."

"What?" I felt like I'd been punched in the gut. "What did she want?"

"She asked to speak to you. I told her you were still in bed."

"Why is she calling?" I asked. After ten years, why was she calling now? I felt the pancakes start to tumble and churn in my stomach.

"She said she's clean; she's done with the drugs," Gram said. "She wants to see you. I told her we'd talk to you about it. You don't have to decide now. I asked her to wait until at least Wednesday before calling back."

I felt the pancakes begin to rise up in my throat. "I'm gonna be sick," I said, jumping up from the table. I ran to the bathroom and threw up my breakfast. I was still hanging over the toilet, with the last bit of thick, gooey spit dangling from my mouth, when I started crying. I didn't realize that Gram and Pap had followed me until Gram started rubbing my back, the way she used to when I was little.

"Are you okay, honey?" she asked.

"I'm all right," I said, grabbing a wad of toilet paper.

Pap was mad. "She ain't got no business calling up and getting Erin all upset like this!"

"Bob—"

"It's okay. I'm okay. It just caught me off guard. Can I be alone for a minute, please?"

Gram closed the bathroom door on their way out. I sat there for a minute or so and then decided a shower might make me feel better.

I put my head under the stream of warm water. It felt good running down my face. I didn't bother washing anything; instead I just stood there in the water, thinking.

I had seen my mother less than three months ago, sitting outside of Walmart, looking like a junkie. There was no way she had been clean then, so at the very most, she could only be a little more than two months clean. I wondered how long people have to be clean before they're normal again, before they can get a job, have a house, and take care of their kids. And do they normally stay clean or do they usually go back to drugs? It suddenly hit me that I didn't know a whole lot about drug addiction. *I should know these things*, I thought, *I should know what to expect.*

I got out of the shower, dried off, and changed into clean clothes. Gram knocked on my bedroom door.

"Come in."

"I know this is a shock for you, Erin. Is there anything I can do?"

"I'm okay, Gram, really. I'm going to think about it for a little while, okay? Then maybe do some homework."

"Okay, honey. Let me know if you need anything."

When she left, I got on the internet to do some research. After two hours of reading about heroin addiction and testimonials from addicts and their families, I opened my nightstand drawer and pulled out a picture that I kept there—a picture of me with my mom and my dad.

Her skin and hair were soft and smooth. She was smiling, and it wasn't one of those fake smiles people do for a picture. She was actually happy, and it showed. I thought again how Gram had said she was a good mom.

I thought about the addicts' testimonials I'd read.

One woman wrote that after a back injury, her doctor prescribed painkillers. By the time he cut off her prescription, she was already addicted. She said the street price of painkillers was high, and she couldn't afford them, so she turned to heroin because it was so much cheaper. She talked about how she had panhandled, stolen, and even sold her body for heroin.

A guy named Don lost his business, his family, and his home. A girl named Sadie was only fifteen the first time she tried heroin; her boyfriend turned her on to it.

Nobody had been able to tell me why or how my mom started using drugs. There was only one person that knew the answer to that and to all my other questions, and that person was my mom. I needed answers.

Gram and Pap were in the living room watching television when I told them. "I've made my decision."

Chapter Twenty-Three

When my mom called back, Gram told her that I would see her, but she'd have to come here. They set a date for that Saturday.

All week long I wondered if I had made a mistake. I'd read those testimonials on the internet, and I felt bad for some of the drug addicts, but the reason I felt bad for them was mainly because they were sorry for what they had done. I didn't know if Mom was sorry at all. For all I knew, she was just lonely, and I was the only person she had left.

After all these years, I was starting to get on with my life. Now, when I was happy, that's when she decided to get clean and wanted to see me? I found myself back where I was a year ago, obsessing over her, and it pissed me off. How could someone I'd spent only five years with, someone who I remembered very little, get to me so much? I didn't want it to bother me, but it did, and it showed. Tuesday during class, while we were supposed to be working on an assignment, George leaned over and quietly asked, "Are you mad at me or something?"

"No, not at all. I just have a lot on my mind. Not anything I want to talk about now though." I knew that I could tell George what was going on, and he wouldn't judge me, but this was something he couldn't understand. His mother and father were both alive and together. From the one time I met his father, I could tell that George's family was normal. Someone with a normal family doesn't get what it's like to live with your dead father's parents because your heroin-addicted mother ditched you when you were five.

"Okay, that's cool," he said, but he didn't look okay. He looked hurt, and the last thing I needed was a guilt-trip because I didn't want to spill my guts. I never thought I could get irritated with George, but I was.

"Look, my mom's a heroin addict. She took off when I was five, I haven't seen her since, and I'm seeing her on Saturday," I blurted out. "So I'm a little stressed, and I don't want to talk about it." I glared at him.

"I said okay!" In a quieter voice he added, "I'm sorry you're upset, but you don't have to bite my head off." The bell rang. Picking up his book bag, he shook his head, and walked out without another word.

Good job, Erin, I thought. I had managed to piss off the guy who I was not only crazy about, but who was one of the few true friends I had. He was one of the rare people on the planet that seemed to actually care about me.

George wasn't the only person I lost my temper with that week. I can't count the number of times I snapped at Gram and Pap, but I think they knew I was having a rough time, so they didn't call me on it. George barely spoke to me the rest of the week. If I said hi to him, he'd reply, or if I asked him a question, he'd answer with as few words as possible. I wished that I hadn't been so snippy with him, but I hoped he would forgive me. I didn't want to lose him.

Since George was mad at me, I was glad that Gram and Pap didn't get upset with me too. That would have been too much, even if I did deserve it. Grace didn't suffer the wrath of Angry-Erin that week, simply because she knew what was going on and didn't pry or try to start a conversation. She understood just because I was upset about something didn't mean that I wanted to talk about it; she knew how I felt.

Chapter Twenty-Four

Saturday afternoon, my mom showed up exactly at one o'clock. I was sitting on the porch when a blue Chevy Cruz pulled into the driveway. My mom got out of the passenger side, leaned in, and said something to the lady who was driving. As the car backed out of the driveway, my mom turned toward me. She just stood there, looking at me, not moving a muscle.

I could see her chest expand as she took a deep breath. I watched her walk up the driveway. She didn't look the same as the last time I saw her. Her formerly long, stringy hair had been cut shoulder length and was clean and styled. She was wearing a pair of jeans and a yellow blouse, both of which fit her. She looked pretty—not like she had before the drugs—but still pretty. She got to the end of the sidewalk, standing directly in front of me. "Erin?"

"Yep."

She held out her hand. I could only stare at it. *Seriously? My mother wants to shake my hand?* I thought.

"I'm Maggie, your mother." When she realized that I wasn't going to shake her hand, it dropped to her side.

"I know who you are."

"I didn't know if you'd remember me. It's been a while."

"Gram and Pap have pictures," I said, shrugging my shoulders.

"Can I sit?"

I slid over, motioning to the space on the step beside me. "Go ahead."

She sat down and let out a sigh. Looking down at her hands in her lap, she finally spoke. "Thanks for seeing me. I didn't know if you'd want to or not and wouldn't blame you if you didn't."

"I wasn't sure if I wanted to either."

Neither of us said anything for a minute or two. I finally broke the awkward silence. "You didn't even know who I was."

She looked at me, puzzled. "What?"

"I saw you at Walmart in December. You looked right at my face, right in my eyes, and you didn't even recognize your own daughter."

Her gaze shifted back to her lap. "December...I was still using." She motioned toward the house with her head. "Did your grandparents tell you about that...the drug use?"

"Of course. They kind of didn't have a choice. When you've got a little kid who's been crying for a year nonstop, you gotta give her some sort of explanation. 'Mommy can't come get you now because she's sick.' Eventually they had to explain what 'sick' meant, and that Mommy might not be coming back at all. So, yeah, I know." I'd promised myself I wouldn't cry, but the memory of it was starting to choke me up.

"Erin, I was sick. I am sick. But I'm trying to get better."

"You didn't even know who I was."

"I understand, and I'm sorry. I'm so, so sorry. I know saying it isn't enough. I realize that, but I hope that you know that I mean it. I mean it...I'm *really* sorry." This time, it was her voice that was cracking with emotion.

I was glad that she was sorry. I wanted her to miss me like I had missed her. I wanted her to love me like I loved her. I wanted her to feel bad for leaving. I wanted her to feel at least some of the sadness that I'd felt so deeply and for so long after she left. I wanted her to feel something, *anything* about me.

"Why did you leave?" The million-dollar question.

"Drugs," she said, and then paused. "Heroin."

"That doesn't answer my question. I know you were...are...a drug addict, but not all drug addicts up and leave their kids. Leave their kids to come home from school and sit alone on the porch for hours waiting!" I couldn't help it. I was yelling. "I sat on that porch for hours wondering what I'd done wrong and waiting! Waiting for you to come home, and you never came! Why?"

By that time, I was sobbing.

For a moment, she looked down at her hands as she rubbed them together. She was trembling. When she finally looked up, I saw tears in her eyes. "Erin," she said, trying to put her arms around me.

"No!" I said, pushing her away. "Answer me!"

She looked at me as the tears spilled down her cheeks.

"Answer! I deserve to know! Why did you start? I want the whole story from the beginning."

Her eyes followed a car as it drove by. Then she took a deep breath and began. "A friend, well, someone I was hanging out with, took me to his friend's house one night. You were staying here with your grandparents that night. Some people there were doing drugs. I'd had a few beers. The people seemed okay. They were still functioning and looked normal, and they weren't using needles or anything; they were snorting it. So when they offered me some, I did it."

"And you were hooked...just like that? That quick?"

"Yes and no. Not physically, but I was in love with it from the very first time. When I did it, everything bad went away. I wasn't sad, I wasn't worried, and everything felt...perfect. After your dad died, I was so depressed that I could barely even take care of you, so I started going out, drinking a little, trying to get out of myself some, but none of that helped. I drank, but it didn't make me feel better. It made me sad and drunk. Heroin though...it made me feel wonderful. I'd never felt that good before. I didn't want to go back to feeling bad, so I did it again. And again. And again. Pretty soon, I wasn't doing it for the high. I was doing it because if I didn't, I'd get dope-sick."

"So, what happened on the day that you left?"

"I don't know if you remember, but we didn't have a car. I had gotten the settlement money from your dad's accident, and I told myself that I'd get a car later. I figured we'd done fine without one, so we could wait. Anyway, my friends would either bring the drugs to me, or I'd ride with them to get them. On that day, the regular dealer had been busted, so we couldn't score from him and had to go somewhere else. My friends knew a few places we could try, and we ended up at a guy's house about thirty minutes away. He wasn't a dealer, but he had a direct line to a dealer. So, we waited at his house while his roommate, friend, or whatever the guy was, went and scored." She tossed her hair out of her face, like I had seen her do at Walmart.

"By the time he got back, it was getting close to the time that your bus would come. I thought I'd be getting home a few minutes after you, and that'd be okay, but it didn't turn out that way. I was starting to get dope-sick, so I needed a shot before we left the guy's house. I did it, and then I nodded off. By the time I pulled myself together, my ride had taken the rest of what we'd bought and left me there. Told the guy whose house it was that he was going to the store, and he was taking the heroin with him for safekeeping since I was in no shape to keep track of it. I still had money on me, so the roommate went and got more dope for me. My ride never came back but I had my dope, so I was okay. By the next morning, I was too afraid to come back. I'd left my five-year-old daughter, so I was afraid I'd go to jail."

"Weren't you worried about me? Didn't you even care?" I barely got the words out.

She looked down at her hands again. "This is so hard," she whispered. Then, turning to me with fresh tears, she looked right into my eyes and said, "No."

I felt like I'd been slapped.

"I'm sorry, Erin."

"You said that already," I told her.

"If I could go back and change it, God knows I would. I didn't plan to be like this. It was the most stupid, selfish thing I've ever done, and you don't deserve any of it. I know I can never make it up to you, but I'd like to try. I hope you'll let me."

I wished I hated her. It would be easier.

"You can get up, walk in that house, and never see me again. I wouldn't hold it against you. I have nobody but myself to blame."

Part of me wanted to do just that—walk inside, shut the door, and never see her again.

"Erin, I want to have a relationship with you. You're my daughter, and I love you. I know that sounds like a total load of bullshit, but I hope that over time, I can show you how true it is."

"Why now? Why, all of a sudden, after this many years, did you finally figure out that you supposedly cared about your kid and wanted to get clean?"

She shrugged. "I don't know." After taking a deep breath, she continued. "Actually, that's not completely true. You thought I didn't know who you were at Walmart, and you're partially right. I didn't know it was you, or at least I wasn't sure. Later, I started thinking how messed up it was that my own kid may have walked right by me, and I wouldn't know who she was. I already hated myself to begin with, but it hit me that I used to be a good person, and I wanted to be that person again. I didn't want to live the rest of my life as the junkie who was so screwed up that she didn't even know her own child. I wanted to get clean and get to know you. Try to be a good person again. To be a good mom, even."

"How do I know you won't go back to using? How do I know that you won't disappear again?"

"You don't. And if I promised you it wouldn't happen, I'd be lying to you and lying to myself. There's not a day that goes by that I don't want to use. It's a fight I have to fight every single second of every single day. But it's my fight, not yours or anyone else's, and if I go down, I'm gonna go down swinging. That I can promise. Will you give me a chance?"

"I don't know," I said. After that, we sat in silence until the blue car pulled in the driveway.

"That's my ride," my mom said. "Her name is Jeanine. She's in recovery too. She's letting me stay with her."

"Oh."

"Can I see you again?"

"I don't know. I'll think about it," I said.

"Can I hug you?" she asked.

I wasn't ready for her to touch me. She'd thrown me away ten years ago, and while the little kid in me longed for her touch, the rest of me screamed, *Don't trust her...she'll leave again!*

"I'd rather not," I said.

She looked disappointed. "I understand. I'll call this week to see if you're up for another visit."

When the blue car had pulled away and was no longer in sight, I went inside.

"How'd it go?" Gram asked.

"Okay, I guess."

"What did she have to say for herself?" Pap wanted to know.

"She kept apologizing. She wants to see me again."

"And how do you feel about that?" Gram asked.

"I'm not sure. She's going to call this week. I'll make up my mind after I think about it for a few days."

"She's damn lucky you agreed to see her at all," Pap said. "She's got some nerve, that's for sure."

"You don't have to see her again if you don't want to," Gram said. "How do you feel about seeing her again?"

"Will you freakin' stop!" I was sick of the questions, the comments, and sick of the whole subject.

"Fine," Gram said. Pap didn't say anything. At dinner, the three of us barely spoke at all.

That night after dinner, instead of doing my homework, I went to bed early. I didn't even feel like talking to George or Grace. I needed to think.

As I looked at the swirls, my mind raced. I thought about how great it would be if my mom ended up staying drug-free; how nice it would be to have a relationship with her. Then, I thought about how long it had taken me to finally get to a place in my life where I was happy without her. If I let her back in, and she left again, I'd be devastated. But if I didn't, I might be losing the chance for something I had wanted for so long. Was the risk worth it?

I knew I had a decision to make...and it wasn't going to be easy.

Chapter Twenty-Five

I was slowly climbing the steps of the door to the trailer with a suitcase in my hand. The suitcase was heavy, very heavy, and I was struggling. I set it down to rest my arm. "Hurry up!" someone behind me said.

I turned and replied to my mother, "I can't carry it. It's too heavy."

Her hair was long and greasy, and she was wearing the same clothes she'd been wearing when I'd seen her sitting outside of Walmart. She pushed me aside, grabbed the suitcase, and stomped up to the front door.

"I should've known you wouldn't be able to handle it," she said.

She opened the door, and I followed her in. There were people in our home—dirty, zombie-looking people. They all jumped up, ran to my mother, and pawed at her. "Sit down," she said. "Everyone sit in a circle."

They all dropped into a circle around her. She sat down, placing the suitcase in front of her. None of the dirty people noticed me. Their eyes were on the prize— the suitcase. She slowly opened it as they inched closer. "Back off! Everyone will get a turn," she snapped.

I moved around the outside of the circle until I had a clear view of the suitcase and its contents. It was full of drugs and needles. My mother went around the circle giving a needle to each zombie-person. Then, she held out a needle to me and said, "Here's yours, Erin. I saved the biggest one for you."

I was awakened by the sound of my own voice. "No!"

My eyes flew open and focused on the familiar ceiling swirls. It took me a moment to get my bearings, to realize that I was in my room, I was safe, and I'd had a horrible dream. I'd had plenty of dreams about my mom, mostly when I was little. In those dreams, we were together and happy.

But this dream? Oh, this one was a nightmare, and I felt engulfed by darkness and doom. I knew it was a dream, but I couldn't shake the sick feeling I'd had when my mother offered me heroin. And what she'd said as I struggled with the suitcase. "I should've known you wouldn't be able to handle it."

I sat up in my bed. *It was just a dream,* I said to myself. *There aren't any drugs. There aren't any zombie-people, and even in the dream, I said no.*

I looked at the clock on my phone. It was only five thirty, so I had a little while longer to sleep, but there was no way I was going to risk going back to that dream. By the time I reached the breakfast table, I'd shaken most of the uneasy feeling, but not all. I sat down.

"Well, you're up early," Gram said. "I haven't started breakfast yet."

I shrugged. "I went to bed early, so I woke up early," I said.

I wasn't about to tell Gram or Pap about my nightmare. They'd freak out if they knew that after seeing my mom for the first time in years, I had a nightmare that very same night. I could hear Gram now, "That's no coincidence. I knew seeing your mom would upset you."

There was something I needed to say. "Gram, I know I haven't been the nicest person to be around lately."

"You're right. You haven't," she said.

"I wanted to tell you I'm sorry. I'm going to apologize to Pap too."

"Apology accepted," she said. "Now, how about setting the table for breakfast?"

I got three plates out of the cabinet. "Thanks for not giving me a hard time about it."

"You've had some big changes lately. Changes that would stress anyone, make anyone snippy. But if I were you, I wouldn't make a habit of it. Remember what I said about the cell phone."

I put the silverware, napkins, and glasses on the table and sat down. "Gram?"

"Yeah?"

"I was ugly to George, and now he's barely speaking to me. I don't know what to do."

"Have you tried talking to him?"

"Yeah, but he barely replies."

"Have you apologized?"

"Well...no."

"Why not?"

"I don't know what to say."

"Tell him you're sorry."

"What if he doesn't accept?"

"I think he will. But, Erin, can I say something?"

"Sure."

She sat down at the table beside me. "Ever since you were little, you've had a tendency to be very impatient with people, very short, and sometimes downright mean, like you were that night with the whole 'I want a cell phone' fiasco. You were pushing it yesterday too. With Pap and me, it's one thing; we could put you in time-out or whatever. But that's us. Other people, they don't know what you've been through, so they can't take into consideration why you would act the way you do. You may want to practice thinking before you say things. You don't want your mouth to cause you to lose friends."

I knew she was right. Sometimes I could be pretty hateful. I didn't want to be that way, and I usually didn't realize what I was doing until I'd gone too far. Apparently, it was something I really needed to work on, especially if Gram felt she needed to point it out.

On Monday, during the bus ride to school, I thought about what I'd say to George. Then I thought about it some more in my first two classes. When I walked into the science classroom and saw him sitting in his seat, I still hadn't figured out the right words to say. I sat in my seat, got my book out, and put it on the table in front of me.

"I'm sorry," I said, looking at my book instead of at him.

"What?"

I turned to him. "I said I'm sorry. I'm sorry that I snapped at you last week. I know you're mad, but please don't be anymore."

"Okay...no, wait. It's not okay. I mean, I forgive you but it's not okay. I didn't do anything to you, Erin. You got crappy with me because you were in a bad mood. It sucks what you're going through, but don't treat me like crap when it's really someone else you're mad at."

"I know...you're right, and I promise it won't happen again. Please say we're okay."

"I tell you what, from now on, when you're upset about something, talk to me about it. I care about you. And if you don't feel like talking about it, then don't; but don't jump all over me, either. Deal?"

"Deal," I said.

Chapter Twenty-Six

When I was seven, my teacher's name was Ms. Phillips. She was nice, and I thought she was the second most beautiful lady in the world (my mom was the most beautiful, of course). Ms. Phillips gave me a lot of attention. She let me help her organize things, pass out papers, and sometimes even let me read assignment instructions out loud from the board. Granted, all the kids got to do those things, but when it was my turn, I felt special. "Good job, Erin," she'd say. "Way to go!" My favorite was, "You are one special little girl, Erin."

I'm sure she probably said all those things to the other students too, but that didn't matter; what mattered is that she said those things to me. I felt like I was her most prized student, her best little friend...until one Saturday in the spring, that is.

Pap had some errands to run that day, and he let me tag along. We went to the "orange store," which is what I called Home Depot at the time. On the way back, we stopped at 7-11 where Pap let me pick out some candy for after lunch. I got Mike and Ikes, which were my favorite.

When we got home, I ran into the house and found my Gram sitting in the kitchen with Ms. Phillips. It's always weird to see a teacher outside of school, but it's even weirder to come home and find your teacher at the kitchen table, having coffee with your grandmother.

Instead of being excited, I got really upset. I was hurt, and I was mad. Ms. Phillips was my teacher, my best friend, not Gram's! I threw my box of Mike and Ikes at Gram and ran to my room in tears.

It's actually pretty embarrassing now, but at the time, I felt betrayed. In my seven-year-old mind, I thought they were having a secret friendship behind my back. Of course, that wasn't the case. Gram came in my room and told me that Ms. Phillips was there to see me and to have lunch with us. She said that Ms. Phillips had arrived a few minutes before.

If I hadn't been seven years old, I would have probably felt pretty stupid, but since I was a little kid, all I felt was relief. Gram told me to go straight to the kitchen and apologize to Ms. Phillips, which I did.

I told her, "I'm sorry I was bad," and then, unable to resist setting the record straight, I added, "but you're my friend, Ms. Phillips, not Gram's friend."

Ms. Phillips smiled and said, "Of course I'm your friend, Erin. You're very special to me." After that, we ate peanut butter and jelly sandwiches and potato chips, and then I shared my candy with Ms. Phillips.

I later found out instead of having a traditional parent-teacher conference, Gram had invited Ms. Phillips over to talk and then have lunch afterward. Gram knew how much I liked Ms. Phillips and wanted to surprise me.

Guess that hadn't worked out like she hoped it would, but at least it got straightened out quickly. At the ripe old age of fifteen, I should have handled that type of situation differently, but when something similar happened, I didn't do much better.

I was glad I had apologized to George, because due to an impending blizzard, school was dismissed two hours early. If I hadn't straightened things out with him, I'd be sitting at home, snowed in, stewing over the whole thing.

The first thing I planned to do when I got home was thank Gram and tell her she was right about apologizing to George. She was turning out to be smarter about boys than I'd given her credit for. When I walked into the kitchen, it was kind of like the Ms. Phillips's fiasco all over, but instead of Ms. Phillips, it was my mom sitting at the table with Gram.

Gram looked surprised when I came in. "Erin, why are you home already?" she asked.

"Got out of school early because of the snow," I said. "What are you doing here?" I asked my mom.

"Come sit down, Erin," Mom said.

Here we go, I thought.

"What's going on?" I asked, even though I wasn't sure I really wanted to know. I felt a twinge of the betrayal I'd felt years ago with the Ms. Phillips-affair, but when I remembered how that turned out, I stifled it.

"I came over to see your Gram. I needed to talk to her." As I watched her fidget with her coffee cup, I thought she seemed nervous, and I wondered if she felt that way because of me, Gram, or both of us.

Gram nodded. This was weird.

"About what?" I asked.

"Well, an apology for starters. And to thank her."

"Is that it? When did you get here?" I asked. I wondered if they were up to something. Saying, "I'm sorry" and "thank you" literally takes only four or five seconds.

"Yes, that's all. I got here about an hour ago."

I looked at Gram. She nodded again.

"Y'all have been sitting here for an hour and that's all?"

"Well...yeah, Erin. I wanted to explain things. Just like you deserved to know what happened, your Gram did too."

Gram nodded a third time; that irritated me. I wanted to ask Gram if she'd suddenly gone mute, but then I remembered what she said about thinking before speaking.

"Well, I'm home now. Are y'all done talking or should I go in my room and let you finish?" I asked, trying not to sound like a smart-aleck.

"We're done talking," Gram said.

Ah, her vocal cords are working after all, I thought.

"Since you're home, I'd like to talk to you as well," my mom said.

Gram took her cue, said she had some laundry to tend to, and left us alone in the kitchen. I sat down at the table with my mom.

"I haven't decided if I want you here, so I don't know why you came."

"I was hoping you'd decided, and that your decision was a yes," she said.

I took a breath. I didn't want to get upset when I said what I had to say.

"You threw me away, so you don't get to reappear out of nowhere and expect everything to be all sunshine and rainbows. It doesn't work that way. I've spent the last ten years trying to get over what you did, and the minute I'm finally feeling okay—happy even—you show up and expect me to forget what you did." I was proud of myself because I didn't get choked up.

"I don't expect you to forget anything. I want a chance to make things right. Please, Erin."

"What could you possibly do to make up for abandoning me?"

"Anything I do won't ever be enough. I know that. But I want to try, Erin. I want to be here for you. I want to be what a mom is supposed to be. I want to be someone you can confide in. Someone you can ask for help. Someone who loves you unconditionally. That part won't take any work because I already love you and always will no matter what. But more than anything, I want to prove that to you."

At that moment, she looked so fragile and broken that I felt myself wanting to give in. Then...I did.

"Fine," I said. "One chance."

She grabbed my hand and squeezed it. "Thank you."

"Okay," I said, wondering if I'd just made the stupidest decision of my life.

The doorbell rang. Gram answered the door, and a very pretty, heavyset lady followed her into the kitchen.

"Erin, this is Jeanine," my mom said. "I met her in my N.A., eh, Narcotics Anonymous group."

"Hi, Jeanine," I said. She shook my hand and told me it was nice to meet me.

"Well, we have to get going to our N.A. meeting," Mom said, getting up from the table. "Erin, I'll come see you on Saturday at one o'clock, if that's okay."

I looked at Gram.

"It's fine with me," Gram said.

Before I had a chance to protest, my mom grabbed me and hugged me. "Thank you," she whispered.

When I realized I was hugging her back and it felt good, I had to fight back tears. She let go and walked to the door. At the last minute, she turned to Gram. "Thank you."

When my mom and Jeanine were gone, Gram said, "Well?"

"I told her I'd give her a chance," I said.

"You don't seem very enthusiastic about it."

"I don't want to get my hopes up, you know? I don't know if I can trust her."

Gram squirted some dish soap in the sink and turned on the faucet. "I think she's sincere."

"Yeah," I said, grabbing the coffee mugs from the kitchen table and placing them in the sink. "I believe she's sincere too. But just because she sincerely wants to stay off drugs, doesn't mean she will actually be able to."

"Well, that's true. Let's hope for the best though."

Sometimes, Gram was so optimistic it could be annoying.

"I've got homework to do, so I'm gonna go knock it out now."

"Mmm-hmm," she said, as she squirted more soap into the sink.

I finished my homework and called Grace. I told her all about the conversation with George and then coming home to find my mom and Gram sitting in the kitchen.

"I agreed to give my mom a chance," I finished.

Grace was quiet.

"Are you okay?" I asked.

"Yeah, a little bummed. My mom's birthday is Saturday. We always take flowers to her grave on her birthday and Mother's Day."

I realized I'd been pretty selfish in the past couple of weeks. Actually, I'd probably been selfish our whole friendship. I was always either in the middle of a breakdown or concentrating on something good happening in my life. I was so wrapped up in myself I forgot about the fact that Grace spent every day of her life without her mother.

"Are you still spending the night on Friday?" I asked.

"Yeah, if you still want me to."

"You know I do. What do you want to do? Watch a movie? Play a game? Call boys and hang up on them?" I knew that would get a laugh out of her.

"All of the above," she said.

That night, I dreamed again. Except this time, it wasn't about my mom, and it wasn't bad. This time, it was about George. In the dream, we were sitting on my couch, like we were when he came over, except we were the only people there, and we weren't watching a movie.

We were just sitting. Gram and Pap had gone somewhere. Instead of trying to hold my hand, he kissed me.

The kiss wasn't simply a peck; it was the long-drawn-out kind like in the movies. After the kiss, he said, "I have something to tell you." Right then, I woke up.

I wished I had stayed asleep. I wanted to know what he was going to say. Was he going to tell me he loved me? Or was it something bad? Sure, I could use my imagination to create an ending, but that isn't the same as a dream.

I closed my eyes. I thought maybe if I went back to sleep, I'd get to see how the dream ended. My mind wasn't having any of that nonsense though. I was wide-awake.

I looked at the clock on my phone. It was six o'clock— too early to text George. I suddenly missed him and wanted to talk to him. I wondered if we would ever do anything more than hold hands. I would've liked for him to kiss me, but I wasn't sure about anything beyond that.

I suddenly remembered about the blizzard. When I had fallen asleep, it hadn't even started to snow. I got up and looked out the window. It was coming down hard, and there must have already been half a foot on the ground. I jumped back in my bed and snuggled under the blanket. At some point, I fell asleep again.

When I woke up the second time, it was almost nine. I hadn't dreamt again. I got up and went to the window. It was still snowing. Everything was so white. And it was quiet...very quiet and peaceful, as if every living thing in the world was standing completely still to admire the scenery. I thought about the dream again, about George, and I wondered if he ever dreamed about me. I hoped so.

Chapter Twenty-Seven

We were out of school the whole rest of the week due to the icy roads. Gram said it was a good thing she did the grocery shopping and bought enough to last the whole week. She said snow made everyone hungrier and when icy roads kept people from being able to get to the store, they became ravenous. She called it the diet mentality. "You're never hungry until you go on a diet," she said.

Personally, I would argue the extra eating when it snows is people eating out of boredom because they're stuck in their houses. Thankfully, Grace's dad's truck was four-wheel drive, which meant she could still spend the night on Friday. Since I had already done my homework, I spent most of the first snow day texting George and Grace and looking at Instagram. I thought about telling George that I'd dreamt about him, but he would ask me what my dream was about, and I was too embarrassed to tell him, so I decided against it.

A lot of people on Instagram were posting pictures of their adventures in the snow. There were pictures of snowmen, ice cream made from snow, and dogs in the snow. When I was little, I liked to play in the snow, but not anymore. It was a cold and wet mess. Plus, there was nobody to go outside with.

One of the photos I clicked on had a link to a local news channel where I came across a video that caught my eye. The headline read: MOTHER GRIEVES AFTER LOSING 25-YEAR-OLD SON TO HEROIN OVERDOSE.

This wasn't the first story like this I'd come across. In the video, the news people talked to a police officer, who said there had been six overdoses and one death in their city in less than twelve hours that weekend. He said heroin use was an epidemic and overdose calls were becoming routine. The mother of the 25-year-old said her son had been clean for four years and had relapsed.

If her son had been clean for that long and had relapsed, what were the odds my mom would stay clean forever? The more I thought about that video, the madder I got. How could drug dealers not care people were dying?

They knew what it did to the people that used, but did they even think about people like me? I wished they could see what it did to children of addicts. That they could have seen me at five, on my front porch crying. What about the kids who ended up being orphans because both of their parents were addicts and died from overdoses? I wished I could meet the dealers and the drug manufacturers and tell them I hated them, and I wished they'd die. I also wished I hadn't watched that video.

Grace's dad dropped her off at seven o'clock on Friday. We watched a movie, played cards with Gram and Pap, and then went to my room to hang out. I didn't want to upset her, but I also wanted her to know she could talk to me about stuff. She should count on me the way I could always count on her.

"I don't want to get you feeling sad or anything, but I hope you know if you ever want to talk about your mom, you can always talk to me."

"I know," she said. But she wasn't very convincing.

"I know sometimes I have a tendency to make the world revolve around me, so..."

"It's okay, Erin. Really. I don't even like to think about that stuff, let alone talk about it. Talking about it makes me depressed."

"Well, I wanted to throw it out there."

"Alright, alright, I get it. I promise if I ever feel like I need to talk to anyone about stuff like that, you'll be the first person I go to."

"Thanks," I said.

"Weirdo."

Chapter Twenty-Eight

The next morning, Grace's dad picked her up at ten o'clock so they could go to the flower shop. By then, the main roads were no longer icy, and the stores were open. The grocery store sold flowers, but Grace said her dad wouldn't buy the grocery store flowers for her mom. He'd only buy the ones from the same flower store where he'd always gone to buy her flowers. It was romantic in a sad way.

I felt bad for Mr. Mills. People wait years to find their soul mates. He had found his, and she had died before they got to spend hardly any time together. He would probably always love her. Even if he found someone else to love, would he ever love that person like he loved Grace's mom? I doubted it.

My mom showed up on time. I was a little nervous to see her. This time it was really cold, so I didn't sit outside on the porch waiting for her. When I let her in, Gram came to the door and said hello, but Pap was sitting in the kitchen looking at a magazine and didn't get up.

"Wanna see my room?" I asked.

"Sure." When we were passing the kitchen, my mom saw Pap sitting there and stopped. "Hi, Mr. Whitaker."

He didn't look up from his magazine. "Maggie," was all he said. Not, "Hi, Maggie" or "Hello, Maggie," just "Maggie." I figured he must still be pretty mad at her, and I guess my mom figured so too. Once we were in my room, she said, "When your Pap still liked me, he called me Maggie May, after an old Rod Stewart song."

"Who?" I asked.

"Rod Stewart. He was pretty popular back in the day." She looked around. "Your room is nice."

I had cleaned it that morning. Well, sort of...I put all my dirty clothes in the closet and shut the door. "It's okay," I said.

She walked over to my bookcase, which was crammed full of books. "You like to read, huh?"

"Yeah."

"Your dad was a big reader."

"Gram said he was a writer too."

"Yeah, he was," she said. "He was really good." She got a sad, faraway look on her face. She turned around and looked at me. "You look a lot like him, you know."

"I do?"

"Yeah. A lot of the same mannerisms too," she said and smiled. "When he had something that he wanted to say but didn't know how to say it, his lips would quiver. You know how someone's chin quivers when they're about to cry? That's what his lips did. Yours do the same thing."

I wished I had known the man I shared so many traits with. I wished I could remember him, even a little.

"Do you still miss him?" I asked.

"Yeah. I think I always will. He was really special. And boy, did he worship the ground you walked on." She got that faraway look again. I figured while we were talking serious, I'd go ahead and ask her a question I'd been unable to get out of my head.

"Can I ask you a question?"

She sat down on the bed beside me. "Sure."

"How did you get money for drugs?"

She got quiet for a few seconds before she finally spoke. "Well, at first, I had money from the settlement from your dad's accident. Eventually that ran out." She looked down, and then continued, "After that money was gone, sometimes I panhandled, sometimes I stole, and sometimes I did other things that I'm not proud of. I dated a guy for a year or so. He was a lot older than me, and he was pretty well off. He supported my habit for a while, but he didn't do drugs himself. My habit got more and more expensive. Eventually he got tired of it and of me."

"Older? How old?"

"He was sixty-five."

"Gross," I said before I realized I was saying it.

She didn't seem offended. She actually chuckled a little and nodded. "Yeah, it would seem that way. Really, I was the gross one. I used him and took advantage of him." She grabbed my hand and looked at me. "Seriously though, Erin, everything—*everything*—about that life is gross. It's dark, it's dirty, and if there's a hell—and I believe there is—that's what my life was like."

"But you did that to yourself," I said. "Nobody made you try heroin." I knew it was a mean thing to say, but it was the truth.

She shrugged. "You're right."

Suddenly, I didn't want to talk about it anymore. "What kind of books did my dad like?" I asked.

We stayed in my room and talked the whole time she visited. She asked if I had a boyfriend, and I told her I kind of did. I told her I had a best friend named Grace, and she said she'd like to meet her sometime. I was surprised to find I was actually enjoying spending time with her.

Jeanine pulled into the driveway around three to pick my mom up. We agreed she would come again the next Saturday. When she left, Pap and Gram were in the living room. Gram shouted goodbye, but Pap didn't say anything. I felt kind of bad for my mom, but at least Pap didn't say anything mean to her.

I went to my room and was about to shut the door when I heard Gram say, "You could've spoken, you know."

"I didn't have anything to say," Pap said. "Not after what she did."

"Bob, you have to forgive people. Even if you're not ready to completely forgive her, at least try to be cordial, especially in front of Erin."

"I don't have to forgive anyone, especially not her. I loved her and even treated her like a daughter, and what did I get for it? She disappears and takes Erin with her, and then when she's tired of being a mother, she abandons my five-year-old grandbaby on the front porch.

I don't forgive her. I'll try to be polite for Erin's sake, but Erin's the only reason I'll be polite. I won't forgive her though. I can't. I don't trust her as far as I can throw her."

I understood why he felt that way, and honestly, I didn't trust her much, either.

Grace called shortly after my mom was gone. I barely got a chance to say hello when she said, "Ask Gram if you can spend the night. My dad said it's okay. He'll even come and pick you up."

We never did the overnight thing two nights in a row, but Grace had gone to her mother's grave that day, so maybe she was feeling down and needed me. I ended up staying over at her house, but she never mentioned the visit to her mom's grave. I think she wanted company to keep her mind off it.

Chapter Twenty-Nine

I was glad to go back to school on Monday. It was nice to have snow days, but it got boring after the first two days. Plus, I was happy to see George. I had been thinking about asking Gram and Pap if he could come over for a movie one Saturday night, but before I had the chance, he surprised me.

"Hey, my mom said you can come over one weekend and hang out. We can watch a movie."

"Your mom knows who I am?"

George chuckled. "Well, yeah. I had to tell her who you were so I could ask to invite you over. I was thinking this Saturday?"

I tried to play it cool. "Um, sure...Saturday sounds good."

"I have to warn you though, we'll probably have to watch two movies. The first one will be *The Lion King*, because my mom will make us watch it with my little brother."

"How old is he?"

"He's four. And I'm pretty sure he's seen *The Lion King* five hundred times. Hope you don't mind."

"Are you kidding? It's a great movie! I've seen it four or five hundred times myself."

"Good, but don't say I didn't warn you. He can be pretty annoying."

I thought having a little brother or sister would be awesome.

George's invitation wasn't the only surprise that day. Mr. Thompson stopped me on my way out of English class.

"Erin, can I see you for a sec?"

"Sure, Mr. Thompson."

Grace gave me an "uh-oh" look. "Text me later."

Mr. Thompson grinned at me. He had something green on his front tooth. "I read your story, and I think it's excellent."

"Thank you." I liked Mr. Thompson a lot, and it made me feel great that he liked my story. *Should I tell him about the thing on his tooth?* I wondered.

"There's a regional writing competition that's held every year. All the schools in the area compete—one story from each school. I shared yours with the rest of the English Department, and we all agreed it's the best we've seen in quite a long time. I'd like for your story to represent the school in the competition. If it's okay with you, of course."

I was stunned. "Wow...I don't know what to say. I mean, yes. I'm just shocked. And excited. Thank you!"

Mr. Thompson laughed. "You're welcome. You deserve it, Erin. You did a fantastic job."

"Oh, uh...Mr. Thompson?"

"Yes?"

I pointed to my front tooth. "You have something right there."

"Ah, spinach for lunch. Thanks," he said and ran his tongue over his teeth.

I was so shocked and excited that, for a moment, I couldn't even remember what my next class was. I couldn't wait to tell Grace, so I sent her a text before class started.

"WTG SMART, WEIRDO, BEST FRIEND!" she texted back.

Next, I sent George the same text, and he replied saying how impressed he was, and that I was incredibly talented like him.

When I got home, Gram wasn't in the kitchen. I ran to the bathroom and sure enough, the door was shut. "Hurry up, Gram," I said, knocking on the door.

"I'm using the bathroom!"

"I know but hurry up! I wanna tell you something."

I paced back and forth in the hallway until I heard the toilet flush. When Gram opened the door, I was standing right there. She jumped, grabbing her chest.

"You startled me!"

I didn't bother waiting for her to regain her composure. "Mr. Thompson picked my story for the regional writing competition!"

"What competition?"

"Our school goes up against other schools. Each school picks one story and submits it. The best story wins the competition! And he picked mine!" I was so excited, I was practically jumping up and down.

"Erin, that's wonderful! I'm so proud of you," she said, beaming. "And Pap is sure going to be proud."

"Don't tell him. I want to tell him."

"I won't, I won't." She hugged me. "You make me so proud!" Then, she pulled away and put her hands on my shoulders. "Your daddy would have been so proud of you too." She put her arms around me again.

"Gram?"

"Yes?"

"My mom said my lips quiver like my dad's used to. Is that true?"

"Come to think of it, yes!" I think I saw tears in her eyes.

Pap stayed late for work and didn't get home until Gram was putting dinner on the table. He'd barely had a chance to sit down when I told him the good news. He was as excited about it as I was. In fact, by the way he reacted, you would have thought I'd been elected the first female president of the United States.

"This calls for a celebration!" he said. Gram and I looked at each other.

"What kind of celebration, Pap?"

"I dunno. Cake! How about cake? Balloons! A party! Something!"

"Cake would be good," I said. "Just cake."

"As soon as I finish eating, I'm going to the grocery store deli and getting a cake! What kind do you want, Erin?" he asked.

I looked at Gram. She nodded at me. I knew she was telling me to go along with it.

"Strawberry would be great," I said.

For what was probably the first time in his entire life, Pap didn't eat until he was about to bust. He finished what was on his plate, said, "I'll be back," and was out the door. Fifteen minutes later, he came in carrying a cake decorated with white icing and blue flowers.

"They didn't have strawberry, and the deli people were already gone so I couldn't get it with your name on it. I wanted it to say 'Congratulations, Erin,'" he said.

"That's okay, Pap. It's perfect." And even though it wasn't strawberry, it sure did taste good.

When I went to bed that night, I looked up at the swirls. Some people hate Mondays, but not me. This Monday had turned out to be a great day. *Now,* I thought, *if only I can dream about George when I fall asleep, it will have been completely perfect.* And I did.

Chapter Thirty

The rest of the week was mostly uneventful. Jimmy Howes went three days in a row without insulting me, which was the longest he'd ever gone. It used to hurt my feelings, but eventually, after remembering a movie Gram and I had seen, I started to feel a little sorry for him.

In the movie, this big kid bullied the smaller kids. The bully's counselor eventually found out that he acted that way because he had a horribly abusive home life. After seeing that movie and remembering what Scott had said about Jimmy's parents divorcing, I wondered if maybe Jimmy was like the kid in the movie. Maybe he had a bad life and that's why he was mean. I couldn't imagine someone acting like that unless they had a reason. I thought maybe instead of hating Jimmy, I should try to be more patient and kinder to him. It wouldn't be easy, but I knew I should try.

That Friday, it was Grace's turn to stay over my house. She said I was driving her nuts with my stressing over going to George's, and we should've skipped our Friday that week.

"You aren't being your regular level of weird," she said. "You are being 'someone needs their meds' weird. Seriously, how can you be so paranoid about tomorrow? You act like you're going to watch a movie at the Bates Motel."

Grace knew I didn't like that movie. I didn't like any scary movies.

"Or maybe his little brother will be standing at the end of the hall with his imaginary friends saying, 'Come play with us.'"

"Shut up. I'm nervous enough as it is."

Grace laughed. "That's what friends are for."

"No, really, what if his mom doesn't like me? What if I say something stupid or—" I stopped cold and grabbed Grace's hand. "Oh no! What if I accidentally fart?"

Grace decided that was the funniest scenario imaginable. She held out her right hand to shake imaginary Mrs. Barnes's hand. "Nice to meet you, Mrs. Barnes. I'm...phhhht...Erin. Oh my gracious, pardon me, I had...phhhht...beans for dinner."

"Stop."

"No, really, what if you do? Wouldn't you just die?"

"No way. I'd blame it on the creepy ghost twins!"

We laughed until our stomachs hurt.

When my mom came the next day, she seemed a little off.

Gram and Pap had gone shopping, so we sat at the kitchen table. I told her about how my story had been picked for the writing competition.

"That's good, Erin. I'm excited for you." She didn't seem very excited.

"Are you okay? You seem kind of down."

"Yeah, I'm fine. I'm feeling a little blue today. It comes and goes." She looked at me. "I'll be okay. Tell me about your story. What's it about?"

"It's a short story about a girl who's a DEA agent."

When I saw the look on her face, I wished I hadn't mentioned DEA.

"Well, I think I can guess what inspired that."

I shouldn't have brought up the story. She was already feeling down, and I'd probably made her feel worse. *I'm starting to care about her,* I thought.

"I'm sorry, Mom. I didn't mean to upset you. I shouldn't have told you."

"Erin," she said, putting her hand on mine. "It's not your place to worry about me and my feelings, and you sure shouldn't feel like you have to tiptoe around me. I did this to myself. There's nobody to blame but me." She looked out the window as if the right words could be found there.

"You don't even realize how what I've done has affected you, do you?" she asked, turning back to me.

"What do you mean?"

"You're a fifteen-year-old girl. You should be writing stories about boys or fashion or whatever it is most fifteen-year-olds are interested in. Instead, you're writing about DEA agents. I did that to you. I don't ever want you to apologize to me again for the way you feel or what you write about."

"Everyone makes mistakes, Mom," I said. *Not at the level you did,* I thought, *but we won't go there.*

"You're a sweet girl. But that's no surprise; you've always been sweet. When you were three or four, you had this teddy bear you wouldn't part with for even a minute. You adored that bear. If you thought I looked sad, you'd come over and hold that bear out to me. You'd say, 'Heah, momma. Heah, hug beah.' And you were persistent. I'd have to take the bear and hug him and say, 'Thank you, Erin. Momma feels much better.' Then you'd snatch him right out of my arms."

I laughed.

"Do you think it would be okay if I read your story sometime?" she asked.

"You really want to?" I asked.

"I do."

"Yeah. Mr. Thompson has it, but I'll ask him to make a copy for me."

"Good. I can't wait. And, hey, do me a favor?"

"Yeah?"

"No worrying about me, okay? You worry about boys, clothes, and things like that. Do that for me?"

"Sure," I said. But I knew I was lying.

Chapter Thirty-One

The first kiss...all girls dream about it. I had been thinking about it for a while. I knew it would be George. I envisioned it happening at a dance or somewhere romantic. I even imagined it being beside a lake with swans even though the only lakes nearby are at the city park where there's a bunch of greedy ducks that chase park visitors.

On Saturday evening, Gram took me to George's house. It was in the second richest neighborhood in the county, Engle Lakes. His house was country-style with a wrap-around porch, hanging baskets, and white rocking chairs. Gram was impressed, but I was starting to feel nervous again.

"What a beautiful home," she said.

"It's big," I replied.

Gram walked me to the door. Introductions were made, and then Gram was on her way.

Mrs. Barnes was only about five feet tall. She looked like a little kid standing next to George and his dad. Although George didn't favor her, the whole family was the same in that there wasn't anything about their physical appearance that was extraordinary. When I'd seen their house, I imagined that George's mom would be the type to wear designer clothes and a lot of expensive jewelry. But nope, she was wearing a blouse and jeans. I liked her immediately.

George's little brother, Buddy, looked like a smaller version of George. Before they'd even invited me in, Buddy grabbed my hand and was pulling me inside. "What's your name?" he asked.

"Erin."

"Come on, Erin," he said, dragging me towards the living room. "We're havin' popcorn. We're watchin' *Lion King*."

"Buddy, she's my guest too," George told him. "Sorry," he said to me.

"I don't mind. He's adorable. He's like a mini-George."

"Lucky kid," George said. "Actually," he whispered, "I was much cuter."

Buddy sat me down at the end of the couch. "Sit here, Erin," he instructed.

"I wanna sit by Erin," George said.

They compromised, and I ended up sitting in the middle. Buddy sat so enthralled throughout *The Lion King* you'd never guess he'd seen it so many times. He held my hand through most of the movie, and more than once, he absent-mindedly wiped his buttery popcorn hands on my jeans.

When the movie was over, Buddy didn't want to leave, so George texted their mom, and Mrs. Barnes magically appeared a few minutes later.

"Buddy, it's bath time. Then bed," she told him.

"I don't want a bath," he said, scooting even closer to me.

"Well, you have to have one."

"I want Erin to do my bath."

"No, Buddy. But you'll get to see Erin again soon. She'll come back, won't you Erin?" she asked.

"Oh, yes, ma'am," I answered. I was glad she liked me enough to invite me back over, even if it was to get Buddy to cooperate.

"Buddy, tell George and Erin goodnight."

Buddy got off the couch and before I knew it, he'd planted a buttery-popcorn kiss right on my mouth and followed it up with, "Night-night, Erin."

"Night, Buddy," George said.

Buddy didn't reply; he just walked away with his mom.

"Dang! Dissed by my four-year-old brother! The little player was making moves on my girlfriend!"

"You better step it up. He's really cute," I said.

While George browsed the DVD collection, I realized (as I wiped the buttery grease off my mouth) I'd technically gotten my first kiss from a four-year-old.

He held up two movies. "Which one?"

"You pick." I hadn't seen either of them, and I didn't care what we watched.

He put in a comedy about a clumsy police duo, but we ended up talking instead of watching the movie.

"So, the story you wrote for the competition, what's it about?"

I gave him a quick summary. He seemed impressed. "Wow, Erin. I'd never be able to think up stuff like that."

"While we're on the subject, you've never told me what you like to do for fun."

"Music. I like music."

"Whaddya mean? Listening to music, writing music, playing music? You gotta be a little more specific."

I realized that although I thought George and I were close, I didn't really know much about him.

"All of the above. I love listening to music. I love playing it. I can sing a little, and I've written a few things, but they're not very good."

"Let me guess. You play guitar?"

"Nope."

"Drums."

"Nope," he said. "Guess again."

"Tambourine?" He shook his head. "Um, I have no idea. I listed the three instruments I know of."

"Piano."

"Oh, wow. Do you have a piano?"

"Yeah, an electric one. It's in the music room."

"The *music room*? You have a music room?"

"Yeah, my dad plays drums, piano, and he messes around with guitar too. Come on, I'll show you."

He led me down the hallway to a room at the end with double doors. It was a big room, like a whole separate living room. There was an electric piano, at least ten guitars hanging on hooks fastened to the wall, and a drum set.

"Those are amplifiers," George said, pointing to what looked like speakers. There was even a microphone in a stand.

"Will you play something?"

"Sure, but just for a sec. Buddy goes to bed early, so we usually don't mess around in here after eight."

He turned the piano on, sat down, and began to play. I didn't know the song. It sounded like some sort of classical music, and it was beautiful. After about thirty seconds, he got up. "Okay, that's all for now." He was blushing.

I was stunned. "Wow, you're really good." I followed him back to the living room.

"Thanks. I've had a lot of practice. I've been playing since I was about three. Buddy is already playing, and he's very good for his age."

"So, what does your mom play?"

He laughed. "She plays cards and board games. That's about it."

I sat on the couch. "You want another soda or something?" he asked.

"No, I'm good." He sat down beside me.

"Hey, don't tell anyone at school I play piano. Guys that play guitar are cool, but guys that play piano...eh, I might get busted on."

"I'd be proud of it if I were you, but I won't tell anyone."

"Thanks. So, tell me about your mom and dad."

It took me by surprise, but I figured since he'd shared something personal with me, the least I could do was reciprocate.

Telling him how my dad died was the easy part because I've never gotten emotional talking about him. When I got to the part about my mom, I condensed the story as much as possible.

"My mom left when I was five. I came home from school one day, and she wasn't there. She went to get heroin and never came back, so I ended up living with my dad's parents. I was sad for a long time, then I was mad for a long time. Just when I started to get a grip on my feelings, she called and said she wanted to see me. She's clean now. It's going okay. I mean, I don't trust her, and I worry about her. I'm afraid she'll relapse. That's pretty much the whole story."

"Did she do drugs in front of you? I mean, before she left?"

"I don't think so. She spent a lot of time in her room. Sometimes alone, sometimes with her friends. I think they did it in there. I don't remember much except watching cartoons, eating Pop-Tarts, and making my own food a lot. Oh, and our house was dirty. She didn't clean."

"You're lucky."

"What? How do you figure that?"

"No, I mean lucky you don't remember and that you went to live with your grandparents when you were little. My cousin's friend is our age, and both his parents are addicts. He went to live with his grandparents last year, so he's seen some crazy stuff. He's pretty messed up too. He already smokes pot and drinks, and what's really insane is that he used to do it in front of his parents. They didn't even care as long as he stayed out of their way. He misses lots of school and is always getting in trouble when he does show up. So, when I say you're lucky, I mean compared to people like him, that's all."

I'd never thought about it that way. "I guess I am lucky. That's sad about your cousin's friend," I said. "Can we change the subject now? I'm kind of over talking about drugs."

"Sure. Sorry. Go ahead—talk about something else."

"So, what exactly did you tell your mom about me?"

"She knows about you. You know, that we're dating or whatever."

"Oh," I said, trying to act nonchalant. "Cool. So, have you dated a lot of girls?"

"Nope."

"Oh."

"What about you? How many boyfriends have you had?"

"None."

"Hmm," he said.

"But I *have* been kissed, so I'm not a complete amateur," I said.

His face fell. "Oh, really? Anyone I know?"

I smiled. "Your baby brother."

"Oh!" he said with a relieved laugh. "You think you're funny."

"Yes, and incredibly talented too."

"Stop stealing my lines."

For a moment, we sat there in an awkward silence, neither of us looking at the other. Finally, he said, "Hey..."

"Yeah?" I said, turning to him. He leaned over and gave me a quick kiss.

"Thanks," I said, feeling my ears get hot. I had imagined that kiss so many times, and even though we were awkward and clumsy, it was even better than I'd imagined, because it was real.

"You're welcome," he said.

"That was the best second-first-kiss ever," I told him. My ears were on fire by then.

"So, I guess you're saying I'm a better kisser than Buddy?"

"Yeah, his kisses are slobbery. But don't tell him I said that."

"I won't." Then he leaned in and kissed me again. This time, it wasn't awkward.

Later in bed, I thought about him saying I was lucky, and I realized how different things could have ended up. If my mom had stayed, I might be like George's cousin. Things wouldn't be the way they were now. I wouldn't have been in the same school district as George and Grace, which meant I would have never met them. I wouldn't have gotten my very first kiss from an adorable little kid; I wouldn't have received my true first kiss from George; and there's no way I would have felt as happy as I was feeling. George was right; I was lucky.

Chapter Thirty-Two

"You can tell the second first kiss story to your kids one day!" Grace said.

"What if I don't marry George? Should I still tell them?"

Grace rolled her eyes. "Yeah, and be sure to tell them that you were a smart-aleck too. You don't have a romantic bone in your body, you know."

I laughed. Grace had enough romantic bones in her body for the whole school, and I told her so.

"I think I'm the right amount of romantic," I said. "We need to find you a boyfriend so you can channel your romantic energy into him instead of into me."

"I've got some prospects," she said, shrugging. "I don't understand how come you aren't more excited about George. I would be."

"I am excited. But I'm also a little worried," I said.

"What do you mean?"

"Everything is going so good. I've got you and George. Mr. Thompson picked my story for the competition. My mom is clean and back in my life, and I'm actually starting to care about her. I'm waiting for the other shoe to drop, I guess. Especially when it comes to my mom. I keep seeing news stories about people overdosing. Apparently, a lot of dealers are putting that fentanyl stuff in the heroin. What if she relapses and ends up with heroin that's got that in it? She could die."

"You can't do anything about what she does or doesn't do," Grace said.

"I know, but I still worry. And I'm ashamed of some of the thoughts that have gone through my head. Awful things. Before she got clean, I wished she would just overdose and die. I actually wished for that. And then the other night, I was thinking about how I wouldn't have met you and George if she hadn't been on drugs. I actually saw a bright side to my mom being an addict. How screwed up is that?"

"She deserted you when you were five. You were forced to find a bright side. And so far as wishing death and having messed up thoughts, I get it. When my mom was sick, she was sick for a long time. I remember when she was doing chemo and her hair fell out. I had a bad dream. Usually I'd get up and run to her room when I had a bad dream, but this time, I couldn't because in my dream, she was the monster. She was bald and scary looking. I never told her I had a bad dream that night. I never told anyone." Grace looked ashamed.

"Anyway, she was sick for so long, and I knew she was dying. The last year, she looked a bit worse every day, and it was obvious she wasn't going to get better. So, I secretly wished it would happen. And it wasn't because I didn't want her to suffer; it was because I wanted it done. I still feel guilty about that and about the dream."

"Do you think about it a lot?" I asked.

"Yeah. I wish I didn't. It would be nice to be normal. I wonder what it's like to not have this bad stuff creep into your mind all the time. Sometimes, I look at everyone at school and wonder what kind of stuff they've got going on in their heads that won't leave them alone."

"Me too," I said. "I used to think it was only me, then I met you. I think Jimmy Howes probably has his own stuff. I don't think George does. I think he's normal, which is scary because what happens when he realizes that I'm completely abnormal?"

"Ummm, he probably already knows. I've known since day one. Hence, the nickname 'weirdo.'"

"Oh, yeah, good point," I said.

A couple of weeks passed, and I filled my time with Grace, George, and my mom while I waited to find out if I'd won the contest. I told everyone I didn't care whether or not I won, but that was a lie. I really wanted to win. There were fifteen other schools in the region, and each school had submitted a story, so I tried not to get my hopes up. Besides, if I did win, then my story would go to the state competition against the winners in the other seven regions. I'd be going up against the best seven stories. My story was good, but I didn't think it was *that* good.

I remembered Mom had asked to read my story, so I asked Mr. Thompson if he would make me a copy. He opened up his briefcase and handed me a report binder.

"Here you go," he said.

I opened it, and there was my story. "Hey, this is typed," I said.

"We couldn't submit the handwritten copy."

"That was nice of you. Thanks, Mr. Thompson."

He laughed. "You're welcome, but I didn't type it. I have an arrangement with the keyboarding teacher. When I have things I need typed, I give it to her."

"I'll bring this back on Monday. I only need it for the weekend."

"No rush. It's also saved on the computer. When I submit it next week, it will go electronically."

"Great. When—"

"They'll announce the results in a couple of weeks," he answered before I finished my question.

"Thanks, Mr. Thompson," I said.

My mom seemed to be doing a lot better than she'd been a couple of weeks ago. She said recovery is a very emotional process and drugs had numbed her feelings, but those feelings didn't go away. They lurked deep inside, and when she got sober, they came back with a vengeance. "I'm supposed to focus on staying clean, but it's hard sometimes because I can't stop thinking about your dad. And the guilt I have over what I did to you."

It was true that what she did is something any decent human being would feel guilty about, and it had to make it hard for her to stay clean. I thought it would have been better for her to be clean for a couple of years and then deal with her guilt. How was she going to make things right with me if she couldn't stay clean because she was eaten up with guilt? She'd said her N.A. group helped, giving her advice based on their experiences. I sure hoped they knew what they were talking about.

Mom loved the story. I watched her read it. She chuckled in some places and looked serious in others. I could figure out where she was in the story by the expressions on her face. When she handed it back, she was choking back tears. "It's wonderful, Erin."

"Thanks, but it's not a sad story, so you're not supposed to cry," I said.

"I was thinking how proud your dad would be."

"Did you ever write?"

"No. I barely made it through English classes. You know how some kids are good at math, some are good at science, some at English? Well, I was good at none of them."

"No way. You had to be good at something."

"Nope. It's the truth. I didn't flunk any subjects, but I wasn't really good at any of them either."

"Did you play music or sing or paint? Anything?"

She laughed. "No, my hidden talent is still hidden, unfortunately. Hopefully, I'll find it one day."

We talked about all kinds of things for the rest of the visit, and I was beginning to realize my mom was smart and funny. Sitting there with her, joking and laughing, made me see her in a different way. I wasn't seeing a drug addict; I was finally starting to get to know her as a person, and even though it scared me to get close to her again, it was starting to happen.

Chapter Thirty-Three

The days of Jimmy Howes torturing me came to an end on Tuesday of the next week. Mr. Thompson split us up into groups of four, and Jimmy was one of the four in my group along with a girl named Tasha and a guy named Frank. Tasha was a shy girl who rarely spoke. Frank was outgoing, and everyone liked him. Our assignment was to discuss a story we'd read and decide what we thought drove the main character. In the story, the main character had murdered his wife, but the story didn't say *why* he did it. I guess the author wanted to leave it up to the reader to figure out why.

"I think he did it because he was afraid she'd leave him," Frank said.

"I think he did it because he was crazy," I said. "He did things crazy people do. Like how he always yelled at himself in the mirror."

Jimmy rolled his eyes.

"Tasha? Why do you think he did it?" Frank asked.

Tasha had been staring at her desk. She glanced up quickly. "He wanted to be left alone," she whispered, immediately resuming the desk staring.

"Jimmy?" Frank said.

"She probably looked and acted like Erin. That's the only solid reason I can come up with," he said.

Nobody said anything. Jimmy and Frank looked at me.

Everything I'd thought about how crappy Jimmy's life might be, how he was probably a jerk because he was hurting...all of that went out the window when he implied someone like me deserved to die. I was furious.

"What is *wrong* with you? What's your problem with me?"

He smiled. "Don't like ya."

"If you don't like me, then stay away from me and leave me alone."

He kept smiling...smirking, really, and didn't say a word.

"Look, I don't know why you're the way you are. I always thought there must be a reason you're a pain. Problems at home, maybe. So, I thought, 'Oh, don't let Jimmy bother you. He's a jerk to you because someone must have always been a jerk to him. Maybe his mom or dad, or both.'"

He wasn't smiling anymore.

"And if that's why, believe me, I get it. But I'm tired of it. Everyone I know has stuff to deal with, and some people have it way worse than you. So stop walking around acting like the world took a big dump on you. The world took a big dump on everyone, so don't think you're special, because you're not."

Jimmy didn't say a word. Frank was wide-eyed, his mouth gaping. Tasha hadn't looked up once, not even for a peek.

By then, Mr. Thompson had walked over. "What's going on, guys?"

"Just a disagreement," I told him. "Can I please switch groups?" I think he could tell I was fuming.

"Sure," he said, looking back and forth between Jimmy and me.

"Thanks," I said, standing. Tasha, of course, didn't look up, and Jimmy was now staring down at his own desk looking defeated. *Good,* I thought.

By Saturday, although I'd had plenty of time to cool off, I was still feeling irritable, so it hit a nerve when my mom came over and said, "I can only stay about thirty minutes. Jeanine wants to try a different meeting this week, and it starts at two. We have to leave by about one thirty."

Jeanine was sitting in the driveway with her car running.

"Seriously? You come see me once a week, and you're only staying thirty minutes? Why'd you even bother coming?"

"Because I want to spend time with you, Erin, even if it could only be for a little while."

"If you wanted to spend time with me, you should have come earlier."

"I couldn't. Jeanine had an appointment to get her oil changed this morning, and she's my ride."

"You could have called a cab."

"I don't have money for a cab. I don't even have a job yet," she said, starting to raise her voice. She had started off apologetic, but I could tell she was getting frustrated.

Instead of easing up though, I pressed harder. "You should have asked Jeanine for the money."

"Jeanine brings me here every Saturday. She lets me stay with her for free. She takes me to meetings, and I eat the food in her house. So, no, I'm not going to ask her for money too," she said, angrily. "Please don't be self-centered."

"Me? Self-centered? I'm not the one who left my kid for ten years. *That* is self-centered."

My jab, aimed to make her feel like crap, seemed to work.

"You're right, what I did was horrible, but I can't go back and change it. Jeanine had somewhere to be this morning, and I don't have money, so I'm sorry. My hands were tied, okay?"

"You couldn't panhandle so you could spend time with your daughter? It wasn't beneath you to panhandle for drugs." As soon the words came out, I knew it was a really messed up thing to say.

My mom stood and started towards Jeanine's car. She stopped halfway, walked back with a determined look on her face, and stood directly in front of me. She was trying not to lose her temper, but I could tell she was pissed.

"I'll be here next Saturday at one," she said. I didn't look at her. "Better yet, I'll call your Gram on Friday to make sure you still want me to come. I love you." This was only the second time she'd told me she loved me since she'd come back into my life, and for a moment, I felt my heart soften.

But for some reason, probably out of just plain meanness, I didn't want to give her the satisfaction of knowing how good it felt to hear her say those words, so instead of telling her I loved her too, I stood there, silently staring at her.

Her eyes filled with tears, then she walked to Jeanine's car, and they left.

"Well, that was quick. Is everything okay?" Gram asked when I came inside.

"Yeah, she had to go to a different meeting today. One that starts earlier." I didn't tell Gram how I'd acted, or the things I'd said.

"Oh. Is George still coming for dinner tonight?"

"Yep." I hadn't spent any time with George outside of class since I went to his house, so I was looking forward to seeing him.

I tried to act normal during dinner even though I couldn't stop thinking about what had happened with my mom earlier. I was trying to justify to myself how I'd acted. Luckily, Gram entertained George with stories about her and Pap's time as circus clowns, so I didn't have to talk a lot.

After dinner, George and I sat in the living room. The television was on, but we weren't watching it. Gram and Pap stayed in the kitchen to clean up and play cards. We'd only been in the living room for a few minutes when I told him about what had happened with my mom that day. I didn't tell him all the things I'd said.

"You should give her a break," he said.

"Are you being serious?" I asked. I couldn't believe he would take her side.

"Well, she doesn't have her own car, Erin. You can't be mad at her because her ride didn't work out the way you wanted."

"Yes, I can and I am. Don't try to make me feel bad."

"I'm not trying to make you feel bad," he said. "I think you're mad for no reason."

"How would you know what my reasons are? You have no idea how I feel. You live in your big house with your nice family, playing music together in your music room! You have no idea."

"You know," he said, getting irritated, "a couple of days ago, you told Jimmy Howes off for acting like a jerk, but now you're acting like him."

He was right. I was mad at the whole world for something my mother had done years ago. I had a right to be mad at her, but I shouldn't have acted that way. I felt ashamed.

"You're right," I said. "I'm sorry I said that about your family."

"And so you know, my family isn't perfect either."

"They're pretty close, George."

"My mom had an affair a couple of years ago," he blurted out. "They're just now getting along again."

I was stunned. "Wow! I'm sorry. I had no idea. I would have never thought..."

"You're the one who told Howes that everybody's got something."

"So, what happened? Why did your mom do that?"

"I don't know details. They don't even know I know. I guess they didn't think I could hear them arguing. I'm pretty sure they went to counseling. I thought for a while they'd end up getting divorced, and I'd have to pick who I wanted to live with. I would've picked my dad, which would've killed my mom. So, no, I don't understand what you've been through, but you've never had to spend your nights listening to your parents fight and wonder what was going to happen to them and to you."

"I'm sorry." I grabbed his hand and kissed him on the cheek. "I'm glad your life hasn't been perfect. Wait, that sounds messed up."

He smiled. "I get what you're trying to say. But, Erin, you really need to think before you open your mouth. You make it hard to be around you sometimes."

Gram had warned me my mouth might drive my friends away, and George had confirmed it was a possibility. I had to find a way to control it. And, as much as I hated to admit it to myself, I knew I owed my mom an apology. I'd only gotten mad because my feelings were hurt, and I had wanted to hurt her right back.

When she left, she'd been upset. What if she had skipped the meeting and gone to do drugs instead? *She wouldn't do that,* I thought. *She's not that weak. Or is she? What if she relapsed and it was my fault? No, Erin, it wouldn't be your fault. It's her fault for doing drugs to begin with.* My mind wouldn't stop. I decided that no matter what, I wouldn't act like that again. It was okay to be upset, but it wasn't okay to be hateful. I didn't want to ever wonder if I was the reason my mom relapsed, so I swore that no matter how mad I was, if she told me she loved me, I'd say it back. I hoped it wasn't too late.

Chapter Thirty-Four

It was second period when the front office lady, Mrs. Pack, came over the intercom. "Good morning, Ms. Harris," she said, "Will you please send Erin Whitaker to the office?"

I looked up at Ms. Harris. Why was I being called to the office? I hadn't done anything wrong that I knew of.

"Go on," she said.

I grabbed my things and was almost to the main office when I realized I was trembling.

"I'm Erin Whitaker. You called me here."

Mrs. Pack looked up through her cat-eye glasses from the computer. "Mr. Kennedy wants to see you. Have a seat on the bench. I'll let him know you're here."

Why did the principal want to see me? Had my mom relapsed and overdosed? If she had, wouldn't Gram and Pap be here? Maybe they didn't know. Who would know to call them, or the school, if something did happen to her? I looked at Mrs. Pack to see if she was looking at me with pity or concern. She wasn't looking at me at all but had gone back to doing whatever she'd been doing on the computer. No clues there.

Just then, Mr. Kennedy came out. "Come on in, Erin."

I followed him to his office. He shut the door and motioned to the chair that sat in front of the glass window to the main office. I sat down and let out a deep breath.

He handed me a piece of paper and sat back in his chair expectantly.

I was trembling so hard that I couldn't hold the paper steady. "What does it say?" I asked.

He gave me a funny look. "Wouldn't you like to read it?"

"I can't," I said. "I'm feeling a little queasy."

"It says your story took first place at regionals. I wanted to personally congratulate you. We're very proud of you."

"What?" I asked, not registering what he'd said. My mind was still on my mom, drugs, and death.

"Your story, Erin. You won. Congratulations."

"Oh," I said. Nothing bad had happened. "Oh!" Then I started laughing like a lunatic. I laughed like that until my sides hurt, and then I started crying.

Mr. Kennedy sat completely still, staring. After a few minutes, he held out a box of tissues. I took five. I blew my nose and wiped my eyes. "I'm sorry."

"Oh, it's fine," he said, giving me his best, I-see-this-type-of-thing-all-the-time look. "It's an honor that would make anyone emotional."

If he only knew, I thought. "Yes, sir. May I go now?"

"Of course. We'd like to announce your win over the PA system tomorrow, if that's all right with you."

"Yes, sir. Thank you," I said, standing up. I tried to hand him the paper.

"That's yours to keep. It's a congratulatory letter. I'm sure your parents will want to frame it."

"Thank you, Mr. Kennedy." I put the letter in my backpack. Mr. Kennedy came around his desk and shook my hand.

"Congratulations again, young lady. Excellent work."

Mr. Thompson must have already known the good news, because he didn't wait for the PA announcement. When English class started, he said, "Class, I have an announcement. Erin's story won first place at regionals. Her story will be going to state."

Everyone clapped, even Jimmy Howes. I'd already told Grace right before class started, but she squealed when Mr. Thompson made the announcement. It felt good, but also embarrassing, to hear the whole class clapping for me. My ears got hot, and I caught myself staring down at my desk. *Like Tasha,* I thought. I wondered if she always felt like I was feeling right then.

I couldn't wait to get home and tell Gram and Pap. George had left school early for an appointment, so I'd tell him later. On the bus ride home, I took the letter out of my backpack. It started with, "Dear Ms. Whitaker," (which was cool because I'd never been addressed that way) and went on to say that the judges unanimously picked my story as the best from all the entries. I wondered if my story was really that good or maybe the other stories weren't very good at all. *It doesn't matter,* I thought. *They liked it and I won!*

It was hard, but I managed to wait until dinner to tell Gram and Pap. I pulled the letter out of my back pocket. "I got a letter from school today," I said, trying to look ashamed.

Gram and Pap gave each other a worried look. Gram held out her hand, and I gave her the letter. I watched her face as she read it. "Oh my gosh! You won!"

Pap looked confused.

"She won the story contest!" Gram told him.

Pap's eyes lit up. "Woo hoo!" He high-fived me. "This calls for a celebration!"

"You don't need to go out and buy cake this time," I said.

"What? No cake?"

"Not this time. I would like to have someone over for dinner on Saturday though."

"Sure thing. We can have cake after dinner on Saturday," he said, winking at me.

"Are you inviting George?" Gram asked.

"Actually, I'd like to ask my mom," I said. They both got quiet. "Is that okay?"

"Yes, it's okay," Gram said. "Isn't it, Bob?" She gave Pap a look that said he better say yes.

"I suppose."

"Thank you both. Oh, Gram, I almost forgot. Mom was supposed to call you this week to see if we're still on for the regular Saturday visit. Has she called yet?"

"Haven't heard from her."

"Well, when she calls, will you ask her to come at dinnertime instead?"

"Sure," Gram said.

I didn't want to push my luck, but I also wanted my mom to meet Grace and George.

"Can Grace and George come too?"

"I don't see why not," Gram said. "Bob?"

"Sure," Pap said. "Pass the salt, please."

After dinner, I texted George, told him I'd won, and he was invited over for a celebration dinner Saturday.

"THAT'S MY GIRL! I'LL BE THERE," he texted back.

I had just sent Grace a text to invite her when Gram knocked on my door. "Yeah?"

Gram opened the door. "Your mom is on the phone. I invited her, and she said she's coming if Jeanine will bring her. I didn't tell her you won. I thought maybe you'd like to tell her."

I remembered the nice things Jeanine did for my mom. "Gram, can Jeanine come too?" Gram sighed.

"Okay. Is there anyone else you want to invite?"

"No, but thank you," I said as Gram handed me the phone.

"Hi, Mom. I'm sorry for how I acted the other day. I was upset. I know it's no excuse, so I'm sorry." I rushed to get it out as fast as possible.

"I understand. Hey, your Gram said I'm invited for dinner on Saturday." There was a note of surprise in her voice.

"Yeah, and Gram said that Jeanine can come. It would be nice to invite her since she's always doing stuff for you."

"That's thoughtful. I'm sure she'd love to come."

"It's to celebrate my first-place win for my story!"

"What? Oh, Erin! I'm so proud of you, but I'm not surprised at all. It's a great story."

"Thanks, Mom."

Dinner was at six o'clock, but I told my mom that she and Jeanine should come at five.

"George and Grace are coming too," I said.

"Is George officially your boyfriend now?" she asked.

"Yep, George is my boyfriend," I said, my heart jumping with happiness to actually hear myself say it out loud. "He's great."

Saturday arrived unusually fast compared to the other special days I'd had to wait for over the past several months. My mom and Jeanine arrived at exactly five o'clock. They offered to help Gram cook.

"No, you all go on into the living room and relax." Gram never wanted help until it was time to set the table or clean up. She said there should only be one cook in the kitchen.

Pap was sitting in his chair watching one of his westerns when we came in. "Hi, Mr. Whitaker," my mom said to Pap. He muted the television and put the remote on the table beside him.

"Hello, Maggie," Pap said.

"Pap, this is Mom's friend Jeanine."

Jeanine shook Pap's hand. "Nice to meet you," she said.

"Nice to meet you too. You all go on and sit down. Don't mind me," he said, picking the remote up and turning the volume up to an annoyingly loud level.

We all sat on the couch, and I got as close to my mom as I could.

"Mom?" I asked.

"Yeah?"

"If anything ever happened...you know, if you needed to get a message to me or something, would anyone know to call Gram?"

"I don't know. Probably not," she said. "I guess I could put an 'in case of emergency' piece of paper in my wallet."

"Thanks," I said, feeling relieved.

Dinner went well. I'd been worried it would be weird with my mom being there, but it wasn't. George and Grace were, well, George and Grace, and everyone loved Gram's Luscious Lasagna. There was a lot of joking and laughing, and even Pap joined in. The conversation got serious when Pap, out of nowhere, asked my mom, "So, what's this program you're in?"

Mom was unfazed. "It's called N.A. which stands for Narcotics Anonymous. It's like A.A., only it's for drugs instead of alcohol."

"Hmph," Pap said. "Does it work?"

"It works if you work it," my mom and Jeanine said simultaneously and then laughed.

"That's a recovery slogan," Jeanine said. "And yes, it works if a person is willing to put in the work to stay clean, and even when they do, relapses can happen. I relapsed three times before I finally stayed clean for more than a few months. It's not an easy road, Mr. Whitaker."

"How long you been clean?" Pap asked.

"Six years last month."

Pap's eyes darted to my mom.

"Maggie is doing really well in her recovery," Jeanine said, smiling at my mom.

Jeanine told Pap all about her addiction, her relapses, and her time in the program.

The rest of us listened with fascination, especially me. It was a miracle after all she'd been through that she was still alive and was doing so well she was able to help other addicts. It made me feel hopeful about my mom.

Then Jeanine said something that almost made me spit my drink out. "There's a program called Narateen you might be interested in, Erin. It's for teenagers who are affected by drug use."

"But, I don't do drugs," I said.

"It's not for teens who do drugs," Mom said. "It's for the teens who are affected by people in their lives who do drugs. My addiction has affected you, Erin."

"I'm fine," I said. It pissed me off they would expect me to take the time to participate in something like that. I wasn't the one who needed help.

Gram got up from the table, and Pap spoke up. "Maggie, Erin gets good grades, and she never gets into any trouble. Hell, she won first place in a big writing contest! I don't think she needs any Airateen."

I gave Pap a grateful look. I did not want to go to a meeting to sit around, cry, and drink hot chocolate with a bunch of depressed strangers.

"It's Narateen," Mom said. "And I know she turned out great, but I also know this hasn't been easy for her."

Grace and George looked uncomfortable. I was embarrassed. Everything had been going great until then.

I wanted the conversation to be over, and I didn't want to embarrass myself any more than I already was, so even though I was still mad, I said, "I'll look into it. It might be interesting."

Just then, Gram walked in with a cake. They'd gotten this one personalized: *Congratulations, Erin! Our 1st Place Storyteller!*

"Cake time!" Gram said.

Thank God, I thought.

Gram set the cake down. "We are so proud of you, Erin. Not for winning, but because every single day you make us proud."

Pap lifted up his glass of iced tea. "To Erin!" he said, giving me a wink.

Everyone held up their glasses and replied, "To Erin!"

Chapter Thirty-Five

Everyone was gone before nine. Gram and I had the kitchen clean by nine-thirty. "So, are you going to look into that teen program?" Gram asked as she loaded the dishwasher.

"Eh, I don't know. It doesn't sound like my kind of thing."

She stopped loading. "It wouldn't hurt to look it up online."

"You think so?" I was surprised. It didn't seem like that would be Gram's kind of thing, either.

"When your dad died, people kept suggesting support groups to me. I wasn't the least bit interested. I thought I would be fine, probably even better, dealing with it on my own—well, Pap and me together. But your Pap kind of keeps to himself about it, so I've never had anyone to talk to who understands what it's like to lose a child. Sometimes I think I should have gone. Or maybe that it's not too late to try it."

I thought about the instant connection I'd had with Grace when we met. Neither of us had our moms, so we understood each other. When I thought George's life was perfect, I didn't feel as close to him as I did once I found out it wasn't. Maybe it would be nice to hang around with people who knew exactly how it felt to worry about whether or not their mom or dad would relapse. It was possible they weren't just a bunch of depressed teenagers; maybe they were like me.

"I'll look it up tonight," I said.

I waited until I was in bed to look it up. I typed "Narateen" in the search bar of my phone, and the website came up.

> *If you're a teen and someone important to you is an addict, you can find support in a Narateen group. Narateen is designed for teen Nar-Anon members. If there isn't a group near you, talk to someone in a Nar-Anon group to ask if they could facilitate a Narateen group.*
>
> *Through group meetings, we learn effective ways of coping, while gaining some peace of mind and hope for a better way to live. We help each other by sharing our experiences, strengths and hope. This way we feel free to say what's on our minds and in our hearts.*
>
> *To protect everyone's anonymity, we only use first names. The names and stories shared in confidence aren't repeated outside of group meetings. You won't be forced to speak, but you can always ask questions after meetings. We*

understand how you feel, so know it's a great relief to learn about more effective ways to cope with this disease. And remember, you're no longer alone.

At the bottom of the page, there were three buttons: *Narateen FAQ*, *Is Narateen for me?* and *Find a Meeting*. I clicked them in order. In the *Is Narateen for me?* section, there were twenty questions. A couple hit home.

Do you have a parent, close friend, or relative whose drug use upsets you?

Check.

Are you afraid to upset someone for fear it will set them off to using drugs?

Check.

Do you believe that no one could possibly understand how you feel?

Check.

Do you ever treat people (teachers, classmates, teammates, etc.) unjustly because you are angry with someone else for using drugs?

Check, check, check.

I was stunned. Apparently, there were people who did know how I felt. I hit the *Find a Meeting* button and put in my zip code. There was a meeting every Sunday at five o'clock. It was in a town fifteen minutes away. After reading and answering "yes" to some of the questions, I knew I wanted to go.

Gram and Pap were still awake, sitting in the kitchen talking. They got quiet when I walked in.

"I decided to try one of those meetings," I said.

"Are you sure?" Pap asked.

"Yeah, I'm sure. They meet on Sundays at five o'clock. Can I go tomorrow?"

"You aren't going because your mom pressured you into going, are you?" Pap asked.

"No, Pap. I went online and read about it. It looks like it might help."

Pap looked a little hurt. "Help? I didn't know you were having problems. You know you can always come to us if something is going on."

"I actually didn't know I had problems, or I would have told you. On the website, they talked about treating people badly when it's not even them you're mad at. I know I say mean things to y'all sometimes, and it's for no reason."

He still looked wounded.

"Plus, there were other things they talked about on there that made me think, 'Hey, that's me.' I'd like to try it."

"If you want to go, we'll take you," he said.

Chapter Thirty-Six

The next evening, at 4:50 p.m., we pulled up in front of the church where the meeting was being held. I took a deep breath to steady my nerves.

I realized that I didn't know how long the meeting would last. "I'm going in to ask someone when you should pick me up. I'll be right back."

When I tried to open the front door of the church, it was locked, so I ran to the car. Gram rolled her window down. "It's locked," I said. "Maybe we're at the wrong place."

"There's another building in the back," Pap said. "Saw it when we pulled in. Lights were on. Get in, and we'll drive 'round back."

Around back, there were a few people standing outside of the double doors. I walked over to them. It was two girls and a guy, all about my age, and they were smoking cigarettes.

"You here for the Narateen meeting?" the guy asked.

"Yeah," I said.

"Go in here, then third door on the right," he said, blowing out cigarette smoke.

"Thanks. Uh, when should I tell my ride to pick me up?"

"Usually ends about six thirty." He put his cigarette, which he'd smoked down to the butt, in his almost empty soda bottle and swirled it around.

"Thanks," I said and ran back to the car.

"Come back at six thirty," I said.

"Okay, honey. Have fun," Gram said.

"I will," I said, thinking fun probably wasn't what I'd be having.

When I walked in, I thought I might be in the wrong room. There were ten people sitting in chairs, talking. None of them were crying. They didn't look sad. In fact, they all looked happy. On a table, there were books and brochures. Some of the books had price tags. I picked up a packet that said "Newcomer Packet" and looked to see if there was a price tag. I hadn't brought any money with me.

"Take one; they're free."

I turned around to see a man in his twenties standing there. He shook my hand.

"I'm Dave. I facilitate the meetings. Welcome."

"Thank you," I said.

"And you are...?"

"Erin."

"Good to meet you, Erin. Take any seat whenever you're ready."

I thanked Dave and sat down in a seat on the back row. The three smokers came in and sat a couple of rows in front of me. I decided that they couldn't be more than a year older than I was. Then I remembered George's cousin's friend whose parents were addicts. I guess if he drank and did drugs and his parents didn't care, why would these guys' parents (assuming they were druggies) care if their kids smoked cigarettes?

A girl wearing a Ramones t-shirt sat in the seat next to me. She looked about sixteen and was wearing tons of black eyeliner. "Hey, I'm Nat," she said. "Haven't seen you before. First time?"

"Yeah. I'm a little nervous."

She laughed. "Don't be. You don't have to talk, and if you do, nobody judges. I guarantee you whatever you say won't be as bad as some of the stuff you'll hear."

Dave rapped the lectern with a gavel, and everyone stopped talking.

"Hi, my name is Dave."

"Hi, Dave," they replied.

"Let's open the meeting with a moment of silence followed by the Serenity Prayer." Everyone was quiet for about ten seconds and when Dave began, "God, grant me the serenity...," the rest of the group joined in, "...to accept the things I cannot change, the courage to change the things I can, and the wisdom to know the difference."

I'll never forget how I felt that first time hearing the Serenity Prayer; I felt like it was written for me.

When he finished the prayer, Dave told us all to please silence our cell phones and refrain from using them during the meeting. Then he asked for newcomers to introduce themselves by first name only. As it turned out, I was the only newcomer.

"I'm Erin."

"Hi, Erin," they all said.

People volunteered to read out of one of the books I didn't have. The cigarette guy and Nat read. Some other people got up and made announcements. I didn't understand anything they were doing up to that point, and I wondered if maybe this wasn't for me after all.

They said something about there being no dues but that they relied on donations. When they started passing the basket around to collect the donations, I started to panic and felt even more like this had been a bad idea. Nat leaned over and whispered, "Don't worry about it. A lot of first-timers don't donate. Heck, sometimes regulars don't."

"Oh, cool.... thanks."

Once the basket had made its way back to Dave, he talked about anonymity and explained only one person could speak at a time—no cross-talk. Then he said, "Last week we had a speaker, so this week, we share. Newcomers," he said, looking at me, "will be offered the opportunity to speak after everyone else has spoken. Our topic today is Anger."

I didn't want to speak. I wouldn't know what to say, and I didn't feel comfortable enough to say anything in front of these people.

The speaking order started in the first row. Every time it was someone's turn to speak, they started with, "Hi, I'm *so-and-so*, and my *insert family member* is a *insert drug* addict," and then everyone would reply, "Hi, *so-and-so*." I figured that part out after the first speaker, so I replied "Hi, *so-and-so*," too.

As soon as I heard William speak, I changed my mind again. I was supposed to be there. Everyone listened to him talk, some people shaking their heads in disgust and some knowingly nodding. His dad was a crack addict, and William was angry about a lot of things, but he talked specifically about what had happened that Friday night. The water at his house got turned off because his dad hadn't paid the bill. With the help of William's grandparents the week before, they'd gotten the electricity turned back on after being without it for almost a week.

By the time everyone had spoken, I realized that Nat was right. These people had gone through much worse than I had. One of the cigarette-smoking girls lived with her grandparents, but from what I could gather, the others still lived with their addict parents. Some of their parents were in recovery, and some were still using. Even though their stories varied, I felt connected to each of them because a lot of what they said described exactly how I felt.

When Nat spoke, I had to fight to keep from crying. Her mom, a heroin addict, had overdosed on Wednesday. Nat had come home from school and found her slumped over with a needle still dangling from her arm. She'd called 911, and the EMTs had gotten there to administer Narcan in time to save her mother. Nat was angry at her mom for overdosing, and she said she was even mad at the EMTs for saving her. This was her mom's seventh overdose.

"She won't stop at lucky number seven," Nat said. "She's gonna do it again and again. I don't want her to die, but she must want to because she won't even try to quit. I'm tired of going through this crap."

I noticed when people spoke, nobody offered advice, and nobody asked questions. "Thanks for sharing," they said, and then it moved along to the next person.

When Nat finished, Dave said, "Erin, would you care to share?"

I hadn't wanted to speak, but by the time Nat was done, I knew I wanted to be a part of this group of people who seemed to care about and understand how each other felt.

I cleared my throat. "Um, my name is Erin, and my mom's a heroin addict."

"Hi, Erin."

"I've been angry for a long time, and I didn't know why. Or maybe I did and didn't really realize it." My voice was trembling. "When I was five, I came home from school one day, and my mom was gone." I looked up. Everyone was staring at me, but I took a deep breath and continued.

"For the longest time, I thought it was because of something I did." I started crying, and they looked at me sympathetically. "I thought it was because I kept bugging her for a puh—"

I couldn't finish the sentence because I was crying too hard to speak. Nat put her arm around my shoulder, and someone handed me a tissue. The only person I'd ever told about blaming myself for my mom leaving was Gram.

Maybe it was nerves, maybe it was all the sad stories I'd heard, or maybe it was a combination of both. Whatever the reason, I was in pieces. But I wasn't crying for myself; I was crying for the little girl on the porch who

I could now envision so clearly. I guess Dave could tell I wasn't going to attempt to finish what I was saying.

"Thanks for sharing, Erin," Dave said. "Thanks, everyone, for a great meeting. Let's have a moment of silence and then close with the Serenity Prayer."

This time for the prayer, everyone gathered in a circle and held hands. I usually hate when strangers touch me, but I already felt like these people were friends.

Dave stopped me when I was walking out. "Erin, please come back. We'd love to see you again."

"I will. It was...I don't feel like I'm the only one anymore."

"Good. That's why we're all here—for each other." He picked up a small, light-blue booklet from the table and handed it to me. "Here, take this."

"Oh, I didn't bring any money. Sorry, I didn't know about the basket."

He laughed. "Nobody knows anything at first. You can pay for this next time if you want. If you don't have money, or even if you have money and don't want to pay for it, that's fine."

"Wow, thanks. I'll pay for it when I come back next week. I'll bring basket money too."

"Okay, but it's not a requirement."

"Thanks. See you next week," I said.

As I walked out, I looked at the book he'd given me. The cover read, *Nar-Anon Blue Booklet*.

"So, how was it?" Gram asked when I got in the car.

"It was great. The people are just like me."

"So, tell us all about it," Gram said, putting her hand on Pap's arm.

"Well, I can't tell you specifics. That's a rule. But I can tell you what happens. We started with a prayer, people read out of a book, and then the leader guy said the topic for the evening was anger. They went around the room, and everyone had a turn talking about anger. Then, at the end, we all held hands and said the prayer again. Everyone was really nice. Oh! And I got a book. It costs a couple of bucks, but he gave it to me and said I can pay next time if I want to. Can I come back next Sunday?"

"Of course you can," Gram said. "I'm glad you liked it."

"Can I have some money for the book and the donation? Like four or five dollars?"

"I think we can swing that," Pap said.

I read the little blue booklet during dinner. Gram asked if it was interesting, so I handed it to her. "Here, you can read it. It's pretty short. I don't understand all of it."

She skimmed through it and handed it back to me. "I imagine it'll all make sense once you go a few more times," she said.

After dinner, I called George and told him about the meeting and how I'd broken down.

"Do you think the meetings will help?" he asked.

"Yeah. I do. The people there are super nice, and they're not judgmental. And some of them...Wow! I thought I had been through some stuff. My life is cake compared to theirs. I'm going next Sunday too."

"I'm glad it didn't suck."

"Oh, and get this...the topic was anger. I was definitely meant to go to that meeting."

"You think it will help you stop being a Howes?" That was the new nickname George had given me. He only used it when I snapped at him for no reason, which I was working on not doing anymore. He'd say, "Alright, Howes," and it put me in check every time. I didn't want him, or anyone else, to have to point out to me that I was being a jerk.

"Actually, I think it will help, smart-aleck. And then you'll have to think of a new nickname for me."

"Nah, I like that one."

Chapter Thirty -Seven

I was excited to tell my mom about Narateen. At the end of my first meeting, Nat had explained to me the difference between the types of meetings, and because they all had a common thread, my mom and I would have something new to talk about; we'd actually have something in common.

"Well, there's A.A. for alcoholics, and there's Al Anon for the adults in families of alcoholics," Nat said. "Then, there's Alateen and that's like Al-Anon but for teens. Same thing with Narateen. You got your N.A., your Nar-Anon, and your Narateen. The meetings are kind of the same, but different. I've been to N.A. meetings, and they're like ours. It's the people who are different because some meetings are for the users, and some are for the loved ones."

"You've been to N.A. meetings?" I asked. Had she done drugs? I couldn't help but wonder.

"Just to see what they're like. To hear it from their side, I guess. Some of the meetings are open, which means anyone can come."

Maybe I'll go with my mom to one, I thought.

Saturday was warm, and I decided to wait for my mom on the porch. That way, when Jeanine pulled in the driveway, I could thank her for suggesting the Narateen meetings. A few minutes before one o'clock, I grabbed some iced tea and one of the bags of chips that Gram packed in Pap's lunches and took them outside with me.

When I was done with the chips, I realized I hadn't brought a napkin to wipe my greasy fingers. I licked my fingers and wiped them on my jeans, which reminded me of Buddy's popcorn hands and made me smile. I looked at my phone; it was five minutes after one. Mom was never late. *Probably traffic,* I thought. I scrolled through Instagram for a few minutes and checked my clock again. She was now fifteen minutes late. I was starting to get worried.

By one thirty, my mind had imagined every possible reason she might be running late, but one word kept jumping out in front—overdose. If she couldn't come or knew she'd be late, she would have called. I opened the front door and shouted in, "Gram, did Mom call?"

"No," she replied.

I shut the front door, sat down on the top step, and checked my phone again—1:40 p.m. Something wasn't right. I stood to go inside and saw Jeanine's car coming down the road. *Thank God,* I thought.

"She better call next time she's running late," I said out loud.

Jeanine pulled into the driveway and turned off the car. I didn't see my mom. Why wasn't my mom in the car? Jeanine got out and started up the walk. The expression on her face said it was bad news. Suddenly, I felt like I'd swallowed a brick.

"Hey, Erin."

"Hey. Where's my mom?"

She looked at me for a moment, and then said, "I don't know, but I don't think it's good. When I woke up this morning, she was gone, her purse was gone, and the money that was in my wallet was gone."

I felt lightheaded, so I sat down. "I don't understand."

"I think she relapsed."

"How? Why? I mean, I thought she was doing really good."

"She was, but relapses happen."

"Why didn't you hide your money? She could overdose! What if she already has?"

"I don't keep a lot of cash in my wallet. There was only twenty bucks in there."

"Sorry," I said. "I know it's not your fault."

"Like I said, Erin, I relapsed three times before I got clean and stayed clean. But even today, I always have to be on guard. It never completely goes away."

"You said she took her purse?" I remembered that she'd said she would put Gram's number as an emergency contact.

"Yeah, I looked around everywhere, and I didn't see it."

"She was going to put something in her wallet with Gram as an emergency contact. Do you know if she did?"

"Actually, she did. We were sitting at my kitchen table when she did it."

Well, at least we hadn't gotten a call saying she'd overdosed...yet.

"What do I do?" I asked Jeanine. My mind had gone blank; I couldn't even think.

"There's nothing you can do. You can't fix her. I think it would do you good to go to a Narateen meeting."

"I already have. I went Sunday."

"So, what did you think?"

"What?" I asked, my mind still reeling. "Oh, I liked it. But I don't think I learned anything yet. At least not anything that would help with this."

Jeanine took my hand in hers. "You do understand that if she did relapse, it has nothing, and I mean nothing, to do with you, right?"

"I know. I've been worried this was going to happen. I'm so scared she'll overdose. Why did she do this? I really, really don't get it. Do you think maybe she'll come back?"

"If she relapsed, and I think she did, she can't come back to my house to stay. She can come and get her things, but she can't stay. I set rules, and she broke the first and most important one. She knew what would happen if she used. And because she stole from me, I doubt she'll have the nerve to come and get her stuff. I wouldn't be surprised if I never hear from her again."

The gravity of the situation hit me, and I began to cry. "Can't you make an exception? I mean, where will she go?"

"Erin, consequences are important when you're dealing with an addict. You set boundaries, and if they cross those boundaries, you have to stay firm even when you hate it. And believe me, I hate it. But she can't come back to stay. If I give in, I'm enabling her addiction. You probably don't understand the concept now, but if you keep going to the meetings, you will."

What happens now? I wondered. *What am I supposed to do?*

"I feel sick," I told Jeanine. "Disgusted and sick."

"Do you want me to go in with you and talk to your grandmother?"

I nodded. Just then, Pap came out with his keys. "I'm running to the hardware store," he told me. Then he asked Jeanine, "Mind moving your car, young lady?"

"Sure," she said, but before she could get down the steps, he asked me, "Hey? Where's your mom?"

"We don't know," I said.

"Never mind. Let's go inside," Pap said, shaking his head. I think he knew what was coming. "Trish!" Pap yelled from the kitchen.

"In the bathroom," Gram yelled back.

When she walked into the kitchen and saw the three of us sitting at the table, she stopped in her tracks. "What's going on?" she asked.

"Maggie took off again," Pap said.

Gram looked at me and then at Jeanine. Jeanine nodded. "She was gone when I got up this morning, and she'd taken the money out of my wallet."

"Do you think...?" Gram asked.

"Yeah, I'm pretty sure," Jeanine said.

"What do we do?" Gram asked.

"There's nothing you can do, Mrs. Whitaker. Simply be here for Erin."

Gram sat down at the table. For a minute, nobody spoke.

Jeanine sighed and picked her keys up from the table. "Well, I wanted to come by and let Erin know what was going on. I'd better get going. N.A. meeting starts soon. Mrs. Whitaker, you can give me your phone number, and if she does show up, I'll call."

Gram ripped off a square from a piece of junk mail and wrote the number on it. I asked Jeanine, "Will you please call me too? Do you have a cell phone? I'll put my number in it." Jeanine pulled a smartphone out of her purse and handed it to me. I put my number in her contacts. "I sent myself a text so I'll have your number," I said.

"Okay," Jeanine said, putting her phone in her purse as she walked to the front door. Then, she stopped at the door, came back, and gave me a hug. "I'm sorry, Erin."

I went to the window and watched until her car was no longer in sight. I wondered where my mom was and who she was with. I imagined her sitting on a dirty, torn couch, putting a needle into her vein and then passing out. One of the junkies would ask, "Are you okay?" but she wouldn't answer, so he'd get a closer look. "Man, I think she OD'd," he would say.

Another junkie would check her pulse. "She's dead; let's get outta here," he'd say. Then they'd all leave her there. They'd leave her there to die alone.

Snap out of it, I thought. *She's not dead. Quit being paranoid.*

I went back into the kitchen where Gram and Pap were still sitting. "I'm going to go lie down for a little while," I said.

"Come here," Pap said. He got up and put his arms around me. "I love you." He held me tight for a minute. "Everything will be okay."

"Thanks, Pap. I'm okay," I lied. "Disappointed and worried, but okay. I guess I've been kind of gearing myself up for this since she came back. I knew it could happen. I really hoped it wouldn't."

As I lay on my bed and thought about the things I'd hoped for, sadness crept in. I'd hoped maybe one day, when she'd been clean for a while, she'd get a job and a place of her own and maybe ask me to come live with her. I'd envisioned her zipping up my dress for the senior prom and being one of those annoying moms who insists on taking a thousand pictures of me with my date before finally letting us leave. I'd imagined someday, all of us—me, Gram, Pap, George, Grace and her dad, my mom, and even Jeanine—sitting down for a big Sunday dinner, laughing, and talking about how, together, we'd made it through the hard times.

Now, those hopes had been stolen from me, and I wondered if I would ever be trusting (or stupid) enough to hope for anything again. The answer to that question came quickly...no, I wouldn't.

Chapter Thirty-Eight

Two hours later, I woke up feeling disoriented. For a few seconds, I wondered if my mom's disappearance had been a dream. It didn't take long to realize it was real.

I sat up, rubbing my eyes. My phone buzzed; someone had texted me. Maybe it was Jeanine. I had three messages waiting: one from George and two from Grace. Normally, I looked forward to getting texts from them, especially George. But that day, the only text I wanted was one from Jeanine saying my mom had come back, and it was all a big misunderstanding. I opened the text from George. He asked me to come over later. I texted him yes, I wanted to. Seeing George might cheer me up.

Grace's texts were, "HEY, WHAT YOU DOING?" and then thirty minutes later, she'd sent, "HELLOOOO? ANYBODY THERE?"

Instead of replying to Grace's texts, I called her. I told her everything that had happened, starting with Jeanine pulling in the driveway without my mom in the car.

"Oh, that sucks," Grace said. "Do you want to come over? My dad won't care. We can order pizza, and I'll bake us some chocolate chip cookies."

"I already told George I'd go to his house."

"Ah, but George won't have pizza and cookies."

"You're trying to make me fat," I said.

"Actually, no. I'm worried about you. That's what best friends do."

"Don't worry about me. I'll be okay." *Mom recently said something like that to me,* I thought.

"I know you will," Grace said. "But call me if you need me."

I felt better after talking to Grace, and by the time I got to George's, I was in a pretty good mood. The three of us (me, George, and Buddy) watched *The Lion King* again, but George and I didn't actually watch it; we talked while Buddy was engrossed in the movie.

George was shocked when I told him about my mom disappearing. "What are you going to do?" he asked.

"According to Jeanine, I do nothing. Just wait, and see what happens."

"Oh. Well, I guess she probably knows more about this stuff than we do."

"I'd kind of like to not talk about it anymore right now. And not because I don't feel like I can talk to you about it. I know I can, but I would rather sit here with you and Buddy and talk about happy things."

"Whatever you want...don't want you getting all Howes on me."

"You can't stop yourself, can you?" I asked.

He smiled and kissed me. "Nope."

I put my head on his shoulder. George made me feel so happy and content.

When the movie ended, George said, "Movie's over, Buddy."

Buddy didn't answer; at some point, he'd fallen asleep. George scooped him up, being careful not to wake him, and whispered, "I'll be right back." Seeing how good George was with Buddy made me think of what a good dad he'd be someday. It also made me think about my dad and how he probably rocked me to sleep when I was a baby.

While George was putting Buddy to bed, I crossed the room to get a closer look at a family photo on the fireplace mantel. George, his mother, and his father stood side-by-side in front of their house. George's mom was holding Buddy, who looked to be about a year old. Looking at those smiling faces, you would never guess there had been any unhappiness in the lives of the Barnes family. I wondered if they were truly happy when that photo was taken or if they were only smiling for the camera.

"What do you wanna do?" George asked when he came back in.

"Whatever you want to do is fine with me."

"TV?"

"Sure."

"What do you wanna watch?"

"How about *The Lion King*?" I asked.

"Funny."

"Anything's fine," I said.

We ended up watching a silly comedy, which was what I needed. I wasn't in the mood for anything serious and hearing George laugh always cheered me up.

When Gram and Pap picked me up, George walked me out to the car and gave me a quick kiss. I don't think Pap saw because he didn't say anything, but I know Gram did because she smiled and winked at me.

"I'll talk to you sometime tomorrow. I'm going to the Narateen meeting, so I'll call or text you before I go."

I was glad that George wasn't just my boyfriend, but also my friend. Being around him and Grace made me feel good. The hard times were always at night, when I was alone in my room, when there was nobody to make me laugh or make me feel safe, nobody to distract me from the things I worried about.

Over the next few weeks, I spent Friday nights with Grace, most Saturday nights with George, and went to Narateen every Sunday. I figured if I stayed busy, I wouldn't think and worry about my mom as much. I was learning a lot at the meetings and had become good friends with Nat; she even spent the night one Saturday. We had fun and also talked about our mothers.

"Can I ask you a question?" I asked.

"Sure."

"What's it like to see your mom doing drugs?"

"I've never actually seen her doing them," Nat said. "I've seen her high more times than I can count, and I've seen her after she's overdosed, with a needle stuck in her arm. So, yeah, I've seen the drugs and paraphernalia, but I've never actually seen her put the needle in her arm. She thinks she's doing something by not shooting up in front of me."

My mouth must have been gaping because she said, "No, really, she thinks that. I guess she figures she qualifies for the Mother-of-the-Year award as long as she doesn't shoot up in front of her teenage daughter."

"Why do you still live with her? Why haven't they taken you away?"

"Oh, I don't live with her. I live with her sister, Aunt Becky. My mom stays there too, but not all the time. She screws up, Aunt Becky kicks her out, she comes back with a bunch of promises, and Aunt Becky lets her back in. Then, the whole cycle repeats. I love my Aunt Becky, but she's a horrible enabler. I've been trying to get her to go to Nar-Anon, but she says with her shift work, it's hard to commit to any kind of scheduled stuff." Nat shrugged.

"Did I hear you right at the meeting? Your mom has overdosed seven times?"

"Yep," she said, nodding her head. "You'd think she would've gotten smart enough or scared enough to stop using. But nope, she keeps on. Idiot."

"I've seen a couple of news articles about addicts dying because they're using heroin that has fentanyl in it. I'm really worried about my mom. Do you think she knows about that fentanyl stuff?"

"Yeah, they know. They like the extra kick they get from it," she said, shrugging.

"They aren't scared?"

Nat made a sad, almost chuckling sound. "My mom is living proof that junkies aren't known for their cautious decision-making skills, Erin."

I knew she wasn't trying to make me feel dumb, but I felt silly and naïve.

"I'm worried my mom is going to die. She just now came back into my life and everything was starting to be good with us; we were starting to get close, I think. I don't want to lose her again, but with this relapse, it feels like I already have. I can't believe she pulled this crap again."

"You can't let it consume you. You've got to live your life. You can't live hers for her too."

"She's my mom..."

"I didn't say you can't love her. Of course you love her. But you have to let her be responsible for herself; it's her life to live, not yours. And worrying? You've gotta give the worries to God...let Him handle the big stuff. You handle the day-to-day-Erin-stuff. I'm telling you, it does get better. Keep coming to the meetings and you'll see. Even if she never quits using, even if she overdoses and dies...and I'm sorry to say it so bluntly, but even then, you can live a happy life. If I can still be somewhat happy after walking in and finding my mom nearly dead with a needle hanging out of her arm, anyone can."

I didn't tell Grace right away that Nat had stayed over. I almost felt like I was betraying Grace by having another friend. That was silly though because Grace would always be my very best friend. When I finally told her, she wasn't mad at all.

"My friend from Narateen stayed over Saturday night," I told her, casually.

"Oh yeah?" she said, not bothering to look up from whatever she was engrossed with on her phone.

"Yeah. You aren't upset, are you?"

"No way," she said, laughing. "Why would I be upset? Did you think I'd be jealous or something?"

"I didn't know. I was hoping not."

"You underestimate my maturity, you know. Plus," she said, tossing her hair back with her hand as if she were a model, "I know that I'm irreplaceable. Nobody will ever be as good of a friend as me."

I was relieved. "You wanna meet her?" I asked.

"Sure!"

"The three of us could have a sleepover. I think you'll like her."

The next Saturday, both Nat and Grace spent the night. The first hour or so was awkward, but once Nat and Grace got comfortable around each other, it was like the three of us had always been friends. We played Monopoly and I won. Both of them jokingly gave me a hard time, saying I'd cheated. We decided we'd do it again soon.

Chapter Thirty-Nine

The month of May rolled around, and it had been two months since I'd heard from or seen my mom. On Sundays, I texted Jeanine to see if she'd heard anything, and each time she sent the same reply, "No, nothing yet."

I thought about my mom and worried about her every day even though I tried really hard not to. I also started praying every night. I didn't know if I was praying right. I'd never done it before, except for the Serenity Prayer at the meetings. A couple of the people at the meetings didn't believe in God, and I wasn't sure if I did either. But surely, if there was a God, and if I prayed, He'd listen, right? Nat had said to give Him my worries, so I did. And little-by-little, I found that I was worrying less each day. I wasn't as consumed with where my mom was and what she might be doing. I prayed she would get clean and stay that way.

On the third Wednesday in May, I came home and both Gram and Pap were sitting at the kitchen table. I wondered why Pap was home early from work; it must not be good.

"Sit down, Erin, we need to talk to you."

From the looks on their faces, I could tell it was serious. I felt my heart sink.

"Your mom came by today," Gram said.

"Is she okay?" I asked.

"Yes, she's okay."

Oh, thank God, I thought, as I breathed a sigh of relief. "Where has she been? What happened?"

"She overdosed, Erin," Gram said.

"What? Where is she now?"

"She's on her way to a rehab in Maryland. It's a church-based center."

"Why didn't she wait for me to get home, so I could say goodbye?"

"She couldn't stay. Her ride to rehab was waiting outside in the driveway. But she asked me to give this to you," Gram said, handing me an envelope.

"I'm gonna go read it in my room," I said.

I sat down on my bed and opened the letter.

Erin,

I want to tell you how sorry I am. I screwed up in a big way. I thought for sure I had this thing kicked, but I was wrong. I shouldn't have come back into your life until I had more clean time under my belt, and I know that now. I guess I was being selfish. I wanted a relationship with you, but I don't deserve that. Not yet.

I'm so glad I've been able to get to know you, my beautiful, talented daughter. If you hate me, I understand, but

I hope you don't, and I hope you will forgive me. I wish I could go back and change everything.

I'll be in rehab for at least a couple of months, hopefully longer. I'll call when I can, and I hope you'll talk to me. Keep writing and doing the things that make you happy.

I love you very, very much.

Mom

I read the letter twice before putting it back in the envelope. "If you never would have tried it to begin with, you wouldn't have to apologize," I said out loud. "How could you be so stupid?"

Gram and Pap were still sitting at the kitchen table when I came back in. "Don't worry," I said. "At least she'll be in a place where there's no drugs."

"It's you we're worried about," Pap said.

"I'm okay, Pap. I promise. I've learned some coping stuff at my meetings, and I've been praying too."

"Well, good," Gram said.

"Nobody your age should have to go to those meetings," Pap said. "What your momma's put you through...it's not right."

"Pap, it's not just me. There are at least fifteen other people in my meetings, and there are probably hundreds more who are my age and going through the same thing right now. You should hear the stories I hear. They're horrible. I'm actually lucky. And most of the reason why is because of y'all. I wish everyone had grandparents like you."

Pap put his head in his hands. He let out a sigh and his shoulders slumped. Then, for the first time ever, I saw him cry. I put my arms around his shoulders.

"Don't cry, Pap. Please don't be sad." I didn't want Pap to cry for me. "I'm okay. I'll be fine, I promise."

Pap didn't say anything, but he hugged me so hard I almost couldn't breathe. Then, it hit me. Pap wasn't only crying for me. He was crying about everything...the loss of his son; his daughter-in-law, who he had loved; his wife, who had for years, quietly dealt with her grief alone; and for the five-year-old girl who'd been found by her neighbors, alone, scared, and crying on her front porch. And yes, he was also crying for his fifteen-year-old granddaughter who had been worrying about things he felt no teenage girl should ever have to worry about.

I held him tight and let him cry.

That Sunday, Nat wasn't at the meeting. I was planning on telling her about my mom when I saw her. I texted her when I got home, but she didn't reply. I was in bed, almost asleep when my phone rang. It was Nat.

"Hey, where were you tonight?" I asked.

"Erin, she's dead. My mom's dead." She wasn't crying. In fact, there was no emotion in her voice at all.

"How?" I asked, even though I already knew the answer.

"Overdose. She took off a few days ago, but she does that all the time, so I didn't think much about it. My aunt got the call yesterday afternoon. She's in pieces."

"What about you?" I asked.

"I haven't completely wrapped my head around it. I haven't even cried. I feel like a walking zombie right now."

"I don't know what to say. I'm really sorry. Do you want to come over tomorrow after school?"

"No, I'm gonna hang out here with my aunt. She's a basket case, so I don't want to leave her alone. We're going to have a service. I'll text you the details once we get it set up, but if you don't want to come, I'll totally understand. It's not like you knew her."

"I'll be there," I said.

"Thanks, Erin. I'll talk to you later, okay?"

I couldn't fall asleep after I got off the phone. I kept thinking it could be me making that call to her instead of the other way around.

I was tired of drugs being the center of my life. Part of me was comforted knowing that my mom cared about me and had wanted a relationship with me, but her coming back into my life came at the cost of a continuous roller coaster ride of emotions. Another part of me wished she had never come back. Sure, I'd had unanswered questions, I'd been sad, and I'd been angry, but all the emotions hadn't come all at once like machine gun fire the way they were now. It was mentally, and starting to become physically, exhausting.

The last time I checked the time, it was 2:04 a.m. When my alarm went off at six, I felt the effects of only four hours of sleep. I got up and went to the kitchen where I knew I'd find Gram. She was making a pot of coffee.

"Nat's mother overdosed last night. She's dead."

"Oh no! That poor girl," Gram said.

"She's gonna text me the funeral service details. Will you take me?"

"Of course."

"Gram, I barely slept at all. Can I stay home from school today? I want to go back to sleep."

"That's fine, honey."

"Thanks. I'm going back to bed," I said.

"Erin?"

"Yeah?"

"I love you."

"Love you too, Gram."

It must have been only thirty seconds from the time I closed my eyes until I fell asleep and the nightmares started.

In the first dream, I walked into the kitchen and found Gram trying to pull a needle out of my mother's arm. My mom was slumped over, but I didn't know if she was nodding off or if she'd overdosed.

"What are you doing?" I asked Gram.

"I'm trying to fix it. But it's stuck." She twisted and pulled.

I shoved her out of the way. "Here, let me do it!"

But when I tried to pull, the needle wouldn't budge. I tried using two hands, but it still wasn't moving.

Gram handed me a pair of pliers. I twisted and pulled and SNAP! The needle broke off, leaving part of it embedded in my mom's vein.

"Well, that's just great," Gram said. "She's a goner for sure, now."

I woke up with a start. *Only a dream,* I thought, and fell right back asleep. In the next dream, I was at the funeral service for Nat's mom. One of the mourners said to a lady beside her, "I've heard of double weddings but not double funerals. I wonder if they got a discount?"

I looked over where the casket was. It was pearl white with gold trim and was as wide as a double bed.

"Come on," Nat said, and I followed her to the casket, already knowing that the extra-wide casket was built for two, and that one of the two lifeless bodies was my mom.

They were wearing identical white dresses, and each had a nametag affixed to the breast area: NAT'S MOM - *R.I.P.* and ERIN'S MOM - *R.I.P.* They could have passed for twins, because in addition to being dressed identically, both of their faces were blue.

"Take your seats, ladies and gentlemen. The show is starting!" shouted a man who looked like Abe Lincoln.

We sat down in the front row, and a lady with frizzy brown hair stood in front of the casket, playing "Yankee Doodle" on a banjo. Two clowns appeared, both juggling bowling pins.

"That's my Gram and Pap!" I said to Nat.

"They're good! Hey, I'm going to get some cotton candy. Be right back."

I woke up and looked around my room. No Abe Lincoln, no banjo player, and no juggling clowns. I looked at the clock. It was after ten thirty.

I put on my clothes, went to the bathroom, and then to the kitchen. Gram wasn't in there. I heard voices coming from outside. Gram and Pap were sitting on the front porch, talking. When I opened the door, Gram said,

"Wow, it's almost eleven. You must have been tired." She scooted over and made a space in between her and Pap.

"Yeah, I was," I said, sitting down between them.

"Feeling better?" Pap asked.

"I guess. Had crazy dreams."

"Bad dreams?" Gram asked.

"I don't remember," I lied. "Only that they were weird."

"Hey, when do you find out about that contest?" Pap asked, changing the subject.

"I think this week."

"Bet you won." Pap was probably already planning celebration number three.

"Doubt it. If I do win though, can we skip the whole celebration thing?"

"What? No celebration?"

"Not this time, Pap. The others were really nice, and I appreciate y'all doing that for me. But, with my mom gone and Nat's mom dying, I'm not in much of a party mood."

"Well, when you win, if you change your mind, say the word," Pap said.

"I will," I said, laying my head on his shoulder.

Chapter Forty

There were more people at Nat's mom's service than I had expected. I thought since she was an addict, she probably didn't have many friends left. Gram and Pap had offered to come in with me, and I was glad they were there because Nat was busy with all the guests. Some of them were around our age, so I guessed they were probably friends of hers from her school.

Even though we had drug-addicted mothers in common, our lives were very different. Nat had never met her father and had always pretty much fended for herself. From the way she acted with her aunt at the funeral, it seemed like maybe Nat not only took care of herself but also took care of her aunt. I'd never taken care of myself or anyone else. Gram and Pap were more like parents than grandparents, so I'd never had to worry about adult things.

Nat had also seen things I'd never seen. I had dreamed about drugs and needles and overdoses, but I'd never seen any of those things in real life. Nat had seen them all. I wondered what other kinds of things she had seen. Sex, maybe? It wouldn't have surprised me. She'd said her mom brought random men to the house as far back as she could remember.

I grabbed Gram's hand and squeezed it. I felt so lucky she and Pap stepped in when my mom stepped out.

The service was only about fifteen minutes. Before we left, I walked up to Nat and gave her a hug. "How are you?"

"I'm good," she said. "Too busy right now to think about anything. I have a feeling it will hit later when everything dies down."

"Well, call me if you need to talk or want to come over."

"I will. Hey...thanks for coming."

I turned around to leave and standing right behind me was Jimmy Howes. "Hi, Erin," he said as he brushed by me and then gave Nat a hug.

"Thanks for coming, Jimmy," she said. She was hugging him hard as if he was a close friend.

How does she know Jimmy Howes? I wondered, as I walked out the door.

Thursday, right before class started, I told Grace about the service for Nat's mother. I wanted to tell her about seeing Jimmy, but before I got a chance, she started crying. Her reaction wasn't what I expected. It wasn't as if this was the first time she was hearing about Nat's mom.

"I'm sorry, Grace. If I knew you'd get so upset, I would have waited until later to tell you."

"It's okay," she said, pulling a tissue out of her purse. She blew her nose and wiped her eyes. "It's not that. There's other stuff going on too."

"What's wrong?" I asked.

"I think my dad has a girlfriend. This morning he told me a friend of his is coming over for dinner Saturday night...a lady friend."

"Maybe you'll like her. Maybe she's nice."

"I know," she said, as she watched her fingers twist and untwist the tissue. "It's just, you know, I miss my mom so much. I feel like if I'm nice to this lady friend of his that I'm letting go of my mom. It's stupid."

"It's not stupid."

"Poor Nat. I feel so bad for her." She looked like she was going to cry again.

"She'll be okay. She's tough," I said.

Grace looked at me. "I don't care how tough someone is. When your mom dies, tough goes out the window," she snapped.

"Grace, Erin, sorry to interrupt your conversation, but class has started," Mr. Thompson said.

"Yes, sir," I said. Grace burst into tears again.

Mr. Thompson asked her if she wanted to go to the guidance office. She gathered up her things and walked out. I didn't pay attention to anything Mr. Thompson said for the rest of class, because all I could think about was Grace, Nat's mom, and my mom. When class was almost over, Mr. Thompson said, "Erin, I'd like to see you after class."

"Is Grace okay?" he asked, when I stopped at his desk on my way out.

"I think so. She's got a lot going on right now."

Mr. Thompson got up, closed the door, grabbed a chair, and put it beside his desk. "Sit, please," he said, motioning to the chair.

"I'll be late for my next class."

"I'll write you a note."

I sat in the chair, putting my book bag on the floor beside me.

"I don't want to get into yours or Grace's business, but she was very upset. And you were in another world during class. What's going on?"

"Well, did you know Grace's mom died when she was ten?"

"No, I didn't know that," he said. "Go on..."

I blurted it all out. "My mom's a heroin addict and because of that, I started going to Narateen meetings. I met a girl named Nat there and now we're friends. I introduced her and Grace, and now they're friends too. Anyway, a few days ago, Nat's mom overdosed and died. Grace and I were talking about it before class. I didn't know it would upset her so badly, or I wouldn't have said anything. Plus, she thinks her dad has a girlfriend, and she's worried about that too."

Mr. Thompson looked dumbfounded. "I had no idea about either of your situations, Erin. I'm really sorry to hear these things." Right then, a look of realization slid over his face. I could tell he just realized why my character, Kit, was a DEA agent.

"Do you live with your mom? And, if I'm getting too personal, tell me and I'll back off."

"You're fine, Mr. Thompson. I'm getting used to talking about it. I've lived with my grandparents since I was five. My mom's in rehab now." I trusted Mr. Thompson, and I knew he wasn't being nosy; he genuinely cared about his students.

"And your dad?" he asked.

"He died when I was two. I don't remember him."

"I'm sorry, Erin." There was an awkward silence, and then he said, "You know, I have to say your grandparents have done an excellent job. And you...I already thought you were a remarkable young lady, and I didn't know what you've gone up against. You should be proud of yourself."

"Thanks, Mr. Thompson," I said. I could feel my ears getting hot and hoped that I wasn't visibly blushing.

He grabbed a slip of paper and scribbled on it. "If you or Grace ever need to talk, I hope you know I'm here to listen." He handed the note to me. "Here's your late slip. You'd better get to your next class."

I stopped in the doorway to ask, "Mr. Thompson, do you know when the contest results will be in?"

"Supposed to be by the end of the week, so I'm thinking no later than tomorrow. As soon as I know something, I'll let you know."

"Okay, thanks," I said. *I hope I win. I could use some good news,* I thought, as I walked to my next class.

As soon as I got home from school, I called Grace. "I'm sorry I upset you. You're not mad at me, are you?" I asked.

"No. I was already upset about this dinner date of my dad's and then when you told me about Nat's mom's funeral, it all just hit me. I don't know why I got so shook. I didn't even know her mom. I guess it brought back all kinds of feelings about my mom. Not your fault. You didn't know I was on the edge." She laughed. "I didn't even realize I was on the edge. Pretty embarrassing, actually, to lose it in front of the whole class."

"Nobody said anything. Not a peep...not even Howes."

"Well, if Jimmy Howes didn't have anything hateful or smartass to say, it's safe to assume that nobody else did. You're still spending the night tomorrow, right?"

"Yep. Oh, and speaking of Jimmy Howes, I didn't get a chance to tell you. He was at the service for Nat's mom."

"Jimmy and Nat are friends? That's weird."

"I thought so too. I think I'll ask her to come over and spend the night with us next Friday, if that's okay with you."

"I could ask my dad if she can stay over here too. I kind of don't want her to be alone," Grace said.

"That's a good idea."

"Hold on, I'm gonna go ask." A minute later, she was back. "He said yes. I'm going to put you on speaker phone while I text her."

We chatted while we waited for an answer. Grace's phone buzzed with a message from Nat asking for a rain check.

"She said her aunt was still having a really rough time, so she wanted to stay with her," Grace told me.

Right after Grace replied to her, I sent Nat a text to ask her if she was coming to the meeting on Sunday. She said she'd be there.

"Well, I'm gonna go try to knock out some homework before dinner," I told Grace. "And I'm sorry for upsetting you earlier."

"Stop apologizing. You didn't do anything wrong. You're always apologizing, and half the time, it's for nothing. Why do you do that?"

"I don't know," I answered. "Habit, maybe?" *Why do I do that?* I wondered. Then aloud, I answered my own question. "Because you're my friend, and I don't want to lose you," I said.

"Well, I wasn't mad and even if I was, I love you, and I'm not going anywhere."

After we hung up, I thought about what Grace said. My mom had said she loved me, but she had ended up leaving. I'd never gotten a chance to apologize about asking for the puppy, and I wondered if my habit of excessive apologizing was a messed up side-effect of the past.

Thanks a lot, Mom, I thought.

After dinner, I did my homework and then called George. We'd worked in groups on a project that day in class, and he'd been put in a different group, so I hadn't been able to talk to him. I told him about the funeral, about how upset Grace had gotten in class, and also about my conversation with Mr. Thompson after class.

"Anything exciting for you today?" I asked, once I realized I had been talking for ten minutes about my friends and myself and hadn't even bothered to ask him how his day was.

"Actually, yes. My dad started a band, and I'm going to be playing keyboard."

"Really? That's awesome. What kind of music?"

"Older rock...like stuff he listened to. Eighties, nineties..."

"So, are y'all gonna play out in public? And will I be able to come watch you?"

"For some stuff, yeah. Some gigs are at bars, and minors can't get in after a certain time."

"But since you're in the band, you get in?"

"Well, they're gonna put the keyboard songs in the first set, so I'll leave after that. I'll be the only band member in history whose mom comes to pick him up to get him home by bedtime. My dad said he doesn't want me out late with them because the later it gets, the drunker and crazier the people get. I won't get paid as much as the other guys, of course."

"You're getting paid?"

"Well, yeah. Oh, and get this...the name of the band is the Carnivores. Isn't that the dumbest band name you've ever heard?"

"It's different. Why'd they name it that?"

"The singer picked it because he likes steak."

"Seriously?"

"Seriously."

"Funny. When can I come see you play?"

"I'll find out from my dad and let you know," he said.

I hoped Gram and Pap would let me go watch him. I could hear Gram now, "There's no way I'm going to drop my fifteen-year-old granddaughter off at a bar!" They'd want to stay. Gram and Pap weren't like *old*, old people, so I wouldn't mind hanging out with them.

Chapter Forty-One

When I walked into English class the next day, Mr. Thompson called me to his desk.

I walked slowly to the front of the room. I had a feeling why he wanted to talk to me, and I wasn't sure I wanted to know.

"The results for the contest came in this morning." He couldn't hold back his smile. "Your story placed second! Congratulations!"

I tried to hide my disappointment. I'd really wanted to win.

"Oh, okay. Thanks," I said, attempting to return his smile.

"They're sending a plaque."

"Okay."

"You look disappointed."

"A little," I said. "I knew I probably wouldn't win, but I was still hoping to."

"Don't look at it that way. Your story was the second best in the whole state. That's quite a feat. And from what I understand, it was a very close second. Be proud of yourself. I'm proud of you."

He was right; second in the whole state was pretty good. *But first would have been better,* I thought.

"You're right. Thanks, Mr. Thompson. I appreciate you picking my story."

"I didn't do it as a favor. I picked it because it was good." I smiled at him and went to my seat. Grace was already sitting in hers.

"Second place," I moaned, as I slid in my seat.

"Huh?"

"My story got second place."

"That's great! Way to go, Erin!" She held up her hand for a high-five, so I high-fived her.

Everyone was excited for my almost-win. George hugged me and said, "Second place at state, first place in my heart." He grinned.

I couldn't help but laugh. "You're such an idiot," I told him.

"I do my best."

"Second place in all of the state? This calls for a celebration!" Pap said when I told him and Gram about the contest.

"Pap, remember I said I wanted to keep it low key? No party this time."

"When did you hear me say anything about a party? I didn't say party. I said celebration. How about we take you somewhere special tomorrow?"

"Where?" I asked. I hoped they weren't thinking of the planetarium or the zoo, or anywhere else I liked to go when I was little.

"It'll be a surprise. You'll see."

Grace's dad was also proud of me. When he referred to Grace and me, he called us "my girls," and that made me feel good. I liked him. I hoped his new girlfriend was nice and Grace would like her. We didn't mention the dinner with his lady friend until we were in Grace's room that night, out of earshot.

"I am dreading this dinner tomorrow," she said. "What if she's one of those women who comes in and acts all nice while my dad's around and then is a witch when he's not looking?"

"I doubt she's a witch. She might be really nice. You should give her a chance."

Grace sighed. "I guess. But what if she is really nice, and I like her a lot?"

"How's that a problem?"

"I'd feel bad, like I'm helping my dad cheat on my mom. I know it's dumb, and I know my mom would want him to be happy."

"It's not like they're getting married. It's dinner."

"Oh, but it could definitely lead to marriage."

I laughed. "For a second, I forgot who I was talking to...the girl who plans weddings within the first ten minutes of hanging out with a guy."

"I'm definitely a planner."

"Speaking of planners, Gram and Pap are taking me somewhere special when they pick me up tomorrow."

"Oh yeah? Where?"

"I have no clue. It's a surprise to celebrate my second-place win. I hope it's not anywhere that has a bounce house or tokens."

"They wouldn't take you to one of those places."

"Um, we're talking about the people who offered to be clowns at my fifteenth birthday party, so anything is possible."

"Good point," Grace said. "Hope you win a lot of tokens."

"If I do, I'll save them for you."

Grace rolled her eyes.

I had another dream that night.

Grace nudged me, waking me up, and when I felt the wet pillow against my face, I realized I'd not only been crying in my dream, I'd been crying for real too.

"I think you were having a bad dream," Grace said. "You were talking in your sleep. Are you okay?"

"I was dreaming about my mom."

"Ohhh. I have those dreams too. They suck," she said.

"I don't remember the whole dream. All I remember is my mom was sitting on our couch watching television, and I asked her, 'Didn't you even miss me?' but she ignored me. I was crying but she didn't even notice. She was too busy watching TV."

Grace put her head on my shoulder and stroked my hair. "My mom used to do this when I got upset. It always made me feel better."

"It's very relaxing," I said.

"Good. Relax and go back to sleep."

"Okay. 'Night, Grace. Love you."

"Love you too." I was asleep within five minutes.

Chapter Forty-Two

Gram and Pap picked me up at noon the next day. "Text me later and tell me how dinner went," I told Grace.

"Definitely."

"So where are we going?" I asked as I got into the car.

"Told you it's a surprise," Pap said.

We drove to the next town. The good shopping centers were on the main road, so when we drove away from the center of town, I couldn't imagine where they were taking me. Pap took a right, and we were in the parking lot of a big, brick building that looked a little like a public library. The sign on the front read: REGIONAL ANIMAL SHELTER. Pap parked the car.

"Why are we here?" I asked, not daring to get excited. Maybe they were bringing me to look...like a cheap version of the zoo.

"You still want a puppy, don't you?" Gram asked.

"What? Are you being for real? You're serious?"

"Yes, ma'am," Pap said.

When we got out of the car, I had to stop myself from running to the door. Gram and Pap were taking their time, and I thought slugs could probably move faster than those two.

When we got inside, there was a lady at the reception desk, eating a celery stick. She put the stick down and with a full mouth asked, "Can I help you?"

"We'd like to look at the dogs, please," Gram said.

She nodded her head to our right, and with her mouth still full, she said, "Down the hall that way. You'll see the signs."

We walked by the first set of cages that housed mostly pit bull-types. I didn't want a big dog. I wanted a dog I could pick up if I needed to; one that could sit on my lap.

We got to a second set of cages in the next room. The dogs in these cages were smaller. There was a beagle, a fluffy dog, and a little scruffy black dog. The beagle was cute but was baying loudly. *Too noisy,* I thought.

At the next cage, I called to the fluffy dog that was licking its paw. "Come here," I said, making kiss sounds. It stopped licking, gave me a disinterested look, and went back to licking.

The little scruffy dog next in line was black and brown with a beard. The hair above its eyes stuck out like bushy eyebrows. It was ugly in a cute way.

When I put my finger through the bars, it sniffed my hand, wagging its tail. I looked at the card on its cage: CHIHUAHUA POODLE MIX - FEMALE - 2 YRS.

"Ah, a girl with bushy eyebrows and a beard," I said. "You won't be getting a lot of dates."

She cocked her head as if to say, "You don't think so?"

"Here's some puppies," Gram called from the end of the opposite row of kennels.

I walked over and looked in. "What are they?"

"The card says they're Dachshund-mix," Gram said.

"They're so cute," I said.

"Would you like one of these?" Gram asked.

"I don't know," I said. "They're cute, but..." I looked back over where the little scruffy dog was. "I'm kind of liking one down there."

Gram and Pap walked with me to the Chihuahua-mix's kennel.

"Oh," Gram said, looking at the card. "A Chihuahua-Poodle mix? Hmm. She's not all that cute, is she?" The dog cocked her head again.

"Hush, Gram. I think she understands you." I put my hand through the cage, petting her head. "I want her."

"I thought you wanted a puppy," Gram said.

"I did. But those puppies are so cute that it won't be hard for them to get adopted. It might be hard for this one. Plus, she's sweet."

Gram sighed. "Okay, let's go up front."

One of the employees put us in a room while she went to get the little dog. When the worker returned and put the dog on the floor, she ignored Gram and Pap and came right to me. I sat on the floor as the black and brown bundle of fur jumped and tried to lick my face. I think she knew she was coming home with me.

"She's not used to other animals and is skittish around young children," the lady said, reading out of a file. "She's fixed, housebroken, weighs ten point two pounds. No behavioral issues. She was surrendered because the family moved and couldn't take her."

I knew right then I'd made the right choice. We'd both been abandoned by people who were supposed to love us and take care of us.

"What's her name?" I asked the lady.

"Don't know. It's not on her card or in her file. Looks like her name will be whatever you pick."

"I want her," I said to Gram and Pap.

"If that's the one you want, that's the one you're getting," Pap said.

The lady took Pap and Gram to fill out the adoption paperwork.

"Can I stay in here with her?" I asked. I didn't want her to have to go back in the cage.

"Sure," the lady said.

When they closed the door, I put my hands under her front legs, so she was on her hind legs facing me. "What shall we name you, sweetie?" She wagged her tail and tried to lick me. "You like Sweetie, huh? Then, Sweetie it is." I hugged her. "I love you, Sweetie. You and me, we're a lot alike. My mom left me when I was young too. I promise I won't ever leave you."

She laid her head on my shoulder, like a little kid would. My eyes welled up.

"What's the matter?" Gram asked when they came back and saw I'd been crying.

"I'm just really happy," I said. "I named her Sweetie."

"Oh, that's a nice name," Gram said. "She does seem like a sweet little thing."

"And she's beautiful too," I said to Sweetie. "You're the most beautiful girl in the world."

"Through a mother's eyes," Gram said, laughing.

The lady gave us a list of suggested items to get from the pet store. Pap offered to drop Gram and Sweetie off at home while he and I went to the store to buy some of the things on the list.

"I don't want to leave her," I told Pap.

"Well, if you trust me and Gram to do it, we'll go in and get the stuff while you and the dog wait in the car."

"Yeah, I trust you."

While we waited, Sweetie jumped down to the floor and sniffed. She jumped back up on the seat and sniffed and then came back to me. She repeated the process at least five more times.

"Well, you're nosy," I said. "I hope Gram and Pap get you some good toys. And don't worry; I won't put dresses on you. I won't put any clothes on you, I promise. And I'll only put cute pictures of you on Instagram." I tried to take her picture with my phone, but she wouldn't be still, so I decided I'd get one later, maybe when she was sleeping.

Gram and Pap came back carrying a bunch of bags and a big box. The big box had a picture of a wire kennel on it.

"Why did you buy her a crate?" I asked. "She doesn't want to be in a crate. She spent a long time caged up."

"We'll only crate her when nobody is going to be home," Pap said.

"Pap, please don't make her go in a cage."

"Erin, dogs like crates. They feel secure in them. Look it up on that fancy phone of yours if you don't believe me."

"Okay, you're right. Cesar says it's okay," I said once I'd looked it up.

"Who's Cesar?" Gram asked.

"The Dog Whisperer," Pap answered. "He's got a television show."

"But she'll only be in it when nobody's home, right?" I asked.

"Only when nobody is home," Pap said.

"Can she sleep with me?"

"Absolutely not!" Gram said, but at the same time, Pap said, "Sure!"

Gram looked at Pap. "A dog does not belong in a bed," she said. "We bought her a little doggie bed, Erin. You can keep it in your room."

"The dog may not even want to sleep in Erin's bed," Pap said. "Let's play it by ear."

"You want to sleep with me, don't you?" I whispered to Sweetie. "Gram, Pap, thank you."

"You're welcome, honey," Gram said.

"Hey, what if I would have gotten third place?"

"We were going to bring you here even if you didn't place at all," Pap said.

"What made you decide to let me get a dog?" I asked.

"Well, you said before that you always wanted one. And with everything that's happened with your mom, we thought now was a good time. Having someone to love and take care of makes life better when you're sad," Gram said.

At that moment, I realized that I had been to Gram and Pap what Sweetie was to me. They'd lost their son and having me to love and take care of had made life more bearable for them. It made me happy to know that me being with them was as good for them as it had been for me.

When we got home, Pap started putting Sweetie's kennel together. Gram started dinner, and I got Sweetie's collar and leash out of one of the pet store bags. She had a pink collar and a matching leash. Gram and Pap had even gotten a tag made for her with her name, our phone number, and address on it. Gram said there was a machine in the store that made the tag.

I took Sweetie out in the backyard. She sniffed around for a good five minutes before she finally peed. Gram and Pap had bought bags for me to pick up after her when she pooped. Gram had given me a good-natured lecture about Sweetie being my responsibility. I was more than happy to feed her, take her out, and clean up after her.

"She peed," I announced when we came back in.

"Thanks for letting us know," Pap said.

By the time dinner was ready, Pap had her kennel together, and I had her food and water dish set out in the kitchen. I'd also taken her bed to my room and put her toys in it. I hoped she'd choose to sleep in my bed instead of hers.

Right before we sat down to eat, I fed her.

"No people food for her. If she comes to the table and begs, we're gonna have to put her in the crate while we eat," Pap said.

Her previous owners must not have fed her from the table because she ate all her food and then headed for the living room. I went to check on her, and she'd settled down on the living room floor. She was licking her paws and wiping her muzzle with them.

"She's grooming herself," I told Gram and Pap as I sat back down to finish dinner.

After dinner, I showed her bed to her. She looked at me and whined. "Aw, you don't want that bed, do you?" I said, picking her up and putting her on my bed. She cried again. After a few minutes of listening to her cry, I asked, "Do you need to go out? Do you have to go potty?"

She cocked her head. I took her outside.

"She pooped," I told Pap when we came back in.

"You don't have to tell us every time she does her business, Erin," Pap said.

"She actually told me that she had to go," I said.

"Oh yeah? What exactly did she say?" Pap asked, looking amused.

I did my best impression of a dog whine.

"Well I guess they weren't pulling our leg about her being housebroken," he said. "That's good."

"She's a good girl," I said, heading back to my room. Sweetie followed me. She knew I was her mom.

Chapter Forty-Three

When my phone buzzed, I was using one of my socks to play tug-of-war with Sweetie. I knew Gram would have a fit if she saw me doing that. She'd say, "That's what we bought the toys for!"

When I answered the phone, Grace said, "This is not good...not good at all."

"Oh no. How awful is she?" I asked, fully expecting Grace to say she was a witch.

"She's not awful; she's great. I mean, really great. I like her a lot."

"So, tell me all about her."

"Well, she's pretty, but not too pretty. You know, not so pretty that she makes you feel ugly when she's around. She's nice to my dad, and I can tell she digs him. She showed up about the time Dad finished cooking. We ate dinner, and she asked me a bunch of questions about school, friends, you know, regular stuff that adults always ask about. Then, after dinner, she helped me clean up. Dad made coffee, and we all went into the living room to sit and chat. Dad stopped in the bathroom first. While he was gone, she saw the picture on the end table—the one of me, my mom, and my dad—and she said, 'Wow, your mom was really pretty,' which you and I both know is true. Then she said, 'I bet you miss her a lot, huh?' So, at that point, I realized she's not going to be one of those women who is jealous of the dead wife. She's actually acknowledging her and saying she was pretty, so I'm liking her a little bit. Then, get this...she said, 'My mom died when I was ten, and I still miss her.' Erin, she's like an older version of me. She gets it."

"That's great, Grace. I thought she might end up being nice. Your dad seems like he wouldn't go for anything other than nice. I think you've seen way too many evil stepmother movies and got convinced they were real. And don't feel bad for liking her. Your mom would want your dad happy. She'd want you happy too."

"I know. But what if I like her and get used to her and then her and my dad break up? That would suck."

"Grace, STOP with the crystal ball crap. You are constantly looking years ahead and worrying about stuff that probably isn't even going to happen. You're not only a planner, you're a worrier."

"I know. I'm gonna work on that. So, where was the mystery place you went to today?"

"Ah, hold on, I'll send you a picture." By then, Sweetie was asleep, so I snapped her picture and sent it to Grace.

"Got it," she said. "What? Is that yours?"

"Yep, her name's Sweetie."

"Oh my gosh, she's adorable! Is she a puppy?"

"No, she's two. She's a Chihuahua-Toy Poodle mix, only ten pounds. And she's super sweet."

"How did this happen?"

"I don't know. Gram and Pap picked me up from your house, and next thing I know, we're pulling into the animal shelter parking lot. They had some puppies, but Sweetie and I clicked. They took me because of all that's going on with my mom. Gram said something about having someone to love and take care of."

"Lucky. Hey, I should ask my dad for a dog. I can't wait to meet Sweetie. Am I still staying over on Friday?"

"Yep. I'll probably ask Nat too."

"Good. So, what does George think about Sweetie?"

"He doesn't know about her yet. I'm going to call him when we're done."

"Okay, I'll talk to you tomorrow," Grace said.

I called George and then texted him the picture of Sweetie. He thought she was cute, and he was happy for me. He invited me over to listen to their band practice the next day.

"Oh, I can't. I have Narateen."

"Well, we are practicing at noon, so we'll be done way before your meeting," he said.

"I hate to leave Sweetie to go to my meeting but I kind of have to, so I don't want to be gone during the day too."

He laughed. "Uh-oh. I'm getting dissed for a dog. I'll probably never see my girlfriend again."

"Wait until you see her in person, and you'll understand why you're getting dissed. Hey, why don't you come over here next Saturday? That way, you can meet her, and I don't have to leave her."

"Love me, love my dog, is it? You put up with Buddy, so I guess I owe ya."

"Yeah, and Sweetie won't ask you to give her a bath or make you watch *The Lion King* five-hundred and seventy-six times."

It was nine o'clock by the time I got off the phone with George. I took Sweetie out and then put her on Pap's lap. "Will you watch her while I jump in the shower?" I asked.

After I showered and put my pajamas on, I went to get Sweetie back from Pap. She was asleep on his lap.

"Fed her, changed her, and now she's napping. Here's your baby back, ma'am," he said, handing her to me. Gram rolled her eyes.

"Thanks, Pap. Goodnight." I kissed him on the top of his head and gave Gram a kiss on the cheek.

I put Sweetie in her bed. "If you don't like that bed, let me know, and I'll bring you up here," I said.

Less than two minutes later, she jumped up on my bed and cuddled up to me. "Good girl," I told her.

That night, I dreamt. I don't remember what I dreamt about, but it wasn't a bad dream. I remember waking up for a moment feeling happy and then feeling even happier when I remembered that Sweetie was with me. I reached over and patted around with my hand until I felt her fur. She was still on the bed but had moved about a foot away. I gave her a pat on the head and went back to sleep.

Chapter Forty-Four

When I got to the meeting on Sunday, Nat was already there sitting in our usual spot. "How are you?" I asked.

"Eh, okay, I guess. My aunt finally stopped crying and right when she stopped, I started. I've been an off-and-on faucet ever since. You know, as mad as my mom made me and as screwed up as she was, I miss her a lot. There were times, not many, but there were times that were good. I remember when she took me to the petting zoo. I think I was about seven. And once, we had a picnic in the front yard with peanut butter and jelly sandwiches. We went to the beach a couple of times too. One time, a jellyfish stung me. It hurt like hell, and I screamed bloody murder and said I never wanted to go back. A week later, I was begging for her to take me to the beach," she said, chuckling.

She got quiet for a moment and then looked at me and said, "I wish things were different." I didn't know how to respond, so I put my arm around her.

"Great," she said, reaching in her pocket and pulling a tissue out. "The faucet's on again."

"I know what you mean. I think about the big 'what if' question all the time, but then I try to think about the good things I would've missed out on if my mom hadn't started using...like you, George, Grace, Gram and Pap. That's the only thing that makes me feel any better."

Trying to change the subject, I said, "Oh, speaking of Grace, she's staying over Friday. You wanna stay too? You'll get to meet my new dog," I said, showing her the picture of Sweetie on my phone.

"You got a dog? That's awesome. I've always wanted a dog. Or a cat even."

Just then, Dave started the meeting. "Hey, how do you know Jimmy?" I whispered.

"We were in a program together," she said. "Can't say what though...the whole anonymity thing, you know."

I wondered what program they were in together. Then, for a moment, I almost felt sorry I'd gone off on him because, apparently, there really was a reason he was a jerk, and if he was in a program for it, it couldn't be good.

When it was Nat's turn to share, she got extremely emotional. I kept thinking how that might be me sitting there one day, trying to talk but not being able to through the sobs. I knew it was a possibility. Things for my mom would end up one of two ways: she'd get clean and stay clean for the rest of her life, or she'd relapse and eventually die.

For all I knew, she could have already relapsed. If she had, it wasn't like she would give me a courtesy call to let me know. I had spent my whole life hanging in the balance, and I knew I would spend the rest of my life that way. Unless, of course, I totally wrote her off like her parents had done.

She'd told me they wanted nothing to do with her. When they found out she was on heroin, they tried to get her into rehab and told her if she didn't go, they'd break all ties with her. She found out the hard way that they meant it. They changed their number and even told her they'd call the cops if she came on their property.

Those people, my other grandparents, were nothing like Gram and Pap. My mom's parents didn't care what happened to me. When they kicked my mom out of their lives, I was kicked out along with her. What kind of people shut out an innocent little kid? I only vaguely remember them. I don't remember what they looked like, and I wouldn't know them if I saw them, but I remember feeling a bad vibe from them. I could tell, even being as young as I was, that they didn't care for me, or probably kids in general.

I wouldn't write her off like her parents did. I loved my mom, and as long as she was trying, I would try to be there for her, even though I'd never fully trust her. If she started using again, I wouldn't allow her in my life, but if she was trying to stay clean, I would. I was learning a lot at the meetings, and one of the most useful things I learned is that I can love my mom, but at the same time, walk away from her if it's unhealthy for me to have a relationship with her. I can set boundaries and if she oversteps them, I don't have to allow her to hang around and screw up my life any more than she already has. Even if I never see her again that doesn't mean that I don't love her.

When I came home from the meeting, I took Sweetie out and fed her. After dinner, we went into my room, and while Sweetie was on my bed getting her belly rubbed, I called George. He asked me how the meeting was.

"Good," I said. "How was band practice?"

"It was a lot of fun. It'll be a couple of months before we're ready to play at any venues. There are a lot of songs to learn."

"I promise I'll come and watch you practice before then. If I'm still invited, that is."

"You know you are."

George told me about the songs they'd practiced and about his fellow band members. He liked them. "They don't treat me like a kid. They cuss and joke in front of me like I'm one of them. I even learned a few dirty jokes. Wanna hear one?"

"No, not really. I'll hold out for actually being there to hear them first-hand."

"Oh, they'll be on good behavior if you're in the room."

"I can't wait."

We talked for a few minutes more, and then I took Sweetie out, gave her a treat, and we went to bed. She snuggled up next to me, and I wondered how anyone could have left such a sweet, good, little dog. I wondered how she felt when they left her at the shelter. Did she know they weren't coming back? Was she sad?

"I love you," I told her. "I know you love me. I can see it on your face. I'm sorry if you were sad when your family left, but I'm your mommy now, and I won't ever leave you. Good mommies don't leave their babies."

The thought of her watching her humans turn their backs on her and walk out of that shelter was heartbreaking; I started crying. The thought of that hurt me more than the memory of myself at five, sitting on my front porch, alone and crying for hours. But I had Sweetie now, and she had me.

Gram was right; having someone to love and take care of made a huge difference. I'd only had Sweetie for a little over a day, and already I knew she was what I needed in my life. I realized even if my mom never got better, I could still be happy. I had Gram and Pap, I had George, Grace, and Nat, and now I had Sweetie. I knew I'd be okay.

Chapter Forty-Five

It was the last week of school when she called. I'd just gotten home when the phone rang. "Erin," Gram called. "Your mom's on the phone."

I picked up the phone cautiously, not sure what I would hear. "Hello?" I said.

"Hi, Erin. How are you?"

"I'm okay. How are you?"

"I'm doing really good. I wanted to hear your voice and let you know I'm okay." There was silence on the line. "Do you hate me?"

"No. I'm not even mad anymore."

"I'm so glad. I know how badly I messed up."

"Yeah, you did. I don't know if I'll ever be able to trust you again, but I definitely don't hate you. What happened? Why did you do it?"

"I wish I could answer that question," she said. "I honestly don't know. It just happened." I heard her choke back a sob. "How have things been with you?"

I knew she was trying to change the subject, and I let her. "Good. I joined Narateen, and I got a dog." Silence.

"Are you there?" I asked.

"I'm here," she said, taking a deep breath. "It made me think of when you were little." Her voice was shaky.

"Oh, and I got second place in the story contest," I said.

"That's fantastic! You probably should have gotten first. But second place...in the state, right?"

"Yeah."

"Wow. I'm impressed. Congratulations." It sounded like she was very happy for me.

"How do you like Narateen?" she asked.

"I like it a lot. I'm learning a bunch of stuff, and I made a new friend."

"Really? Good for you. I'm glad."

I wanted to tell her Nat's mom overdosed and died; that's the kind of thing most people would talk to their moms about—unless their mom was an addict who was trying hard to get clean, so I kept quiet.

"How do you like it there?" I asked.

"It's nice. I'm going to stay here as long as they let me. It could be as long as a year. We have group counseling, individual counseling, and church. We have chores, and we all eat together."

"I'm proud of you, Mom," I said. "I know it's hard."

"Thank you. I have to get off the phone now. It will probably be at least a month before they'll let me call again."

"Okay."

"I'll call when I can...and, Erin?"

"Yeah?"

"I'm glad you got a dog. I love you."

"Love you too, Mom. Bye."

It's been almost a month since that call, so I guess she'll be calling back any day now. I hope she stays the whole year; I think she needs to.

I recently visited Nat at her aunt's house, and while I was there, Jimmy came over to see her. We ended up talking for a while. He opened up to me. Come to find out, Jimmy is in Alateen, and the reason his mother divorced his dad was because his dad is an alcoholic and was hitting her. After she left, he had started using Jimmy as his punching bag. Jimmy said even when his dad was falling-down drunk, he was still smart enough to not hit him anywhere that bruises would show.

I told Jimmy all about my mom, and he seemed to understand. He said he was sorry for how he treated me. After what we shared that day, I have a feeling the two of us are going to end up being good friends. I think I'll even invite him over to hang out with us on a movie night.

Nat's still having a hard time dealing with losing her mom, and she'll probably be sad for a long time, but she's got me, Gram and Pap, and Grace. We're family now, and she's safe with us.

Grace's dad's new girlfriend has been over to their house several times since the first time. I met her on Friday, and she's as great as Grace said. I think Grace is going to be fine.

I went to George's this past Saturday and watched them practice. The old guys didn't tell dirty jokes in front of me, but they did cuss. The band sounded good and I had fun. I'm excited to go to a real show, and believe it or not, so are Gram and Pap.

As for me, I'm happy. If you had asked me a year ago if I'd ever be truly happy, I would have said I doubted it. Sweetie is the best little friend anyone could ask for, and I love her to pieces. I love my family and friends, and they love me too. I also love my mom and always will, even if she doesn't stay clean. But I know my life can't revolve around whether or not she stays clean, and I'm finally beginning to accept that.

I used to think I wanted to be a DEA agent when I grow up. I've changed my mind. I want to be a writer, maybe even a journalist. I want to write about drugs and the people who do them. I want to tell their stories so the world will see them for what they are: everyday, normal people who became addicts because of making stupid choices. The choice to try drugs comes at a high price. Addiction ruins lives and tears families apart. Everyone involved suffers. Take it from me. I know.

I hope some of the stories I write have happy endings because I want people to know there's hope that an addict can get clean, stay that way, and be happy.

If my prayers are answered, and I believe in my heart they will be, my very first happy-ending story will be about my mom.

########

About the Author

Amy Voltaire makes a living as an accountant but spends much of her free time writing. She has always loved to write but it wasn't until the sixth grade when she was invited to attend The Young Author's Conference that she realized she might have a knack for it.

Having grown up in an alcoholic home, she knows firsthand what it feels like to be a teenager with an addicted parent. She wants to share the effect this illness has on others.

To learn more about Amy, visit her Facebook page https://www.facebook.com/AmyVoltaireAuthor/